THE CHARIOTS FLEW THEN AND STILL DO TODAY!

AN EXAMINATION INTO THE INFLUENCE OF ALIEN PRESENCE, SCIENTIFIC EVENTS AND THE ERRONEOUS BELIEFS AND RECORDINGS OF BIBLICAL HISTORY

DR. RON PLEUNE

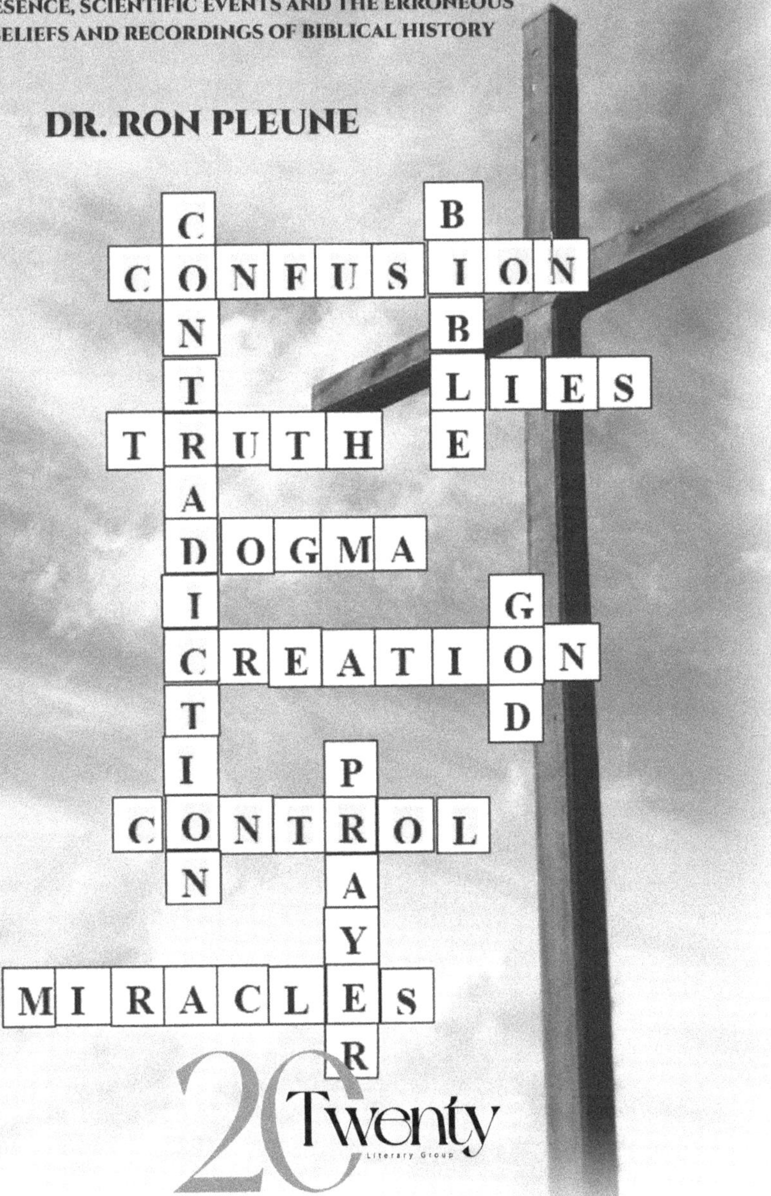

20 Twenty
Literary Group

The Chariots Flew Then And Still Do Today!
Copyright © 2023 by Dr. Ron Pleune

All rights reserved. No part of this publication may be reproduced, distributed, or transmitted in any form or by any means, including photocopying, recording, or other electronic or mechanical methods, without the prior written permission of the author, except in the case of brief quotations embodied in critical reviews and certain other non-commercial uses permitted by copyright law.

ISBN
978-1-961250-59-8 (Paperback)
978-1-961250-60-4 (eBook)
978-1-961250-58-1 (Hardcover)

The Chariots Flew Then And Still Do Today!

TABLE OF CONTENTS

FEAR: WHAT DEITY, IF ANY, IS IN AUTHORITY? HOW DOES IT RULE, AND WHAT IS ITS HISTORY?

As a small child growing up in the 1950s in initially a Methodistbased Christian home, I always thought that there was one god, commonly known as God the Father. Sunday School taught me the love that this God could give, the interaction he had in so called Biblical times as he helped the Hebrews in their life path, and then finally the authority he had over the world and its affairs including mine.

As time marched forward, my family changed denominations to a Baptist Church where my perspective of a God became more defined by the teaching and preaching from what was called the King James Bible.

After a tour in the Navy and several years of college and seminary, I felt called by this God to preach in churches and do campground missionary work. After completing a Bachelor in Business program and a Master's and Doctorate with a major in Apologetics, I felt comfortable in my Christian beliefs and would have stayed in Christianity if I hadn't "looked outside the box" to really understand whether there was a God or not, whether I had been led by this God or not, and where I would fit into His plan.

When my wife and I moved to Utah for six and a half years, I was challenged and at times bothered by how sure the Mormon population was in their belief. After living for several years in Utah, I applied for an adjunct instructor position at a university. I was hired a short time later as the Professor of World Religion which was a great match since I had a Masters' in Religious Education with courses on World Religion, Evangelization and Counseling along with a Doctorate in Religious Education with a major in Apologetics.

You could say that at this time the lid of the box was starting to open up. My position as a professor of World Religion was to "teach" what various major religions believed and not to convert students to Christianity. A portion of each class was devoted to a quiz, questions and discussion regarding the assignment previously given. Before long I began to question my own faith in the Christian Scripture instead of looking through the lens of Conservative dogma. The university moved out of Salt Lake City but the process of examining my faith and the faith of my wife had continued as my wife and I retired from secular employment and moved to my home state of Michigan in the spring of 2015. Life just didn't seem quite right, I continued to question what role the God of Christianity played in directing the affairs of the world when there seemed to be no divine plan because of so much misery, wars, and crime. My questioning went beyond just the present day. It continued as I looked at past history of the world, and it led me to ask what validity is there that creation began roughly at the 4000 BC mark when so much in world history pointed factually to many more thousands of years or even millions of years earlier.

I was beginning to look outside the box, and my mind was ready, for some unknown reason, in December of 2014. I would be introduced to the real truth, the truth of the history of the world, history of the universe, and the history of mankind, which I was to play a unique part in, going forward. The lid of the box was opening, and I could see how I had been led into the box of religion, which stifled my understanding and purpose of life as well as my friends and relations who are still afraid to look outside the box. The journey was about to begin.

In the summer of 2014, while living in Salt Lake City, I picked up a book at a thrift store called *Light Years* by Gary Kinder. It was a documentary of the life and experiences of "Billy" Eduard Meier in Switzerland and his contact with humans from the Pleiades since he was five years old in 1942.

The question that came to mind was "what do they have to do with the God of Christianity?" The question haunted me more and more as my thoughts turned to my own UFO experience in the early summer of 1974 when I witnessed a UFO hovering a few hundred feet above the backyard of the home that my first wife and I had in Rockford, Michigan. My wife witnessed it and a call to the Kent County Airport confirmed that others had seen UFO in the Rockford area also. After approximately ten minutes, the UFO rose higher and higher in the clear blue sky of that Saturday morning sighting until it disappeared.

I was released from the Navy in the spring of 1973, and I went to see a friend of mine by the name of Harry S. who had been a deacon for twenty years in the Baptist Church I was affiliated with at the time. We had talked about UFOs in 1967, at which time he said it was a subject of the devil that tricked the minds of people. I didn't argue with him about it and let it go.

When I knocked on the door of his residence, he gladly invited me in, and he asked me to sit down right away. He said he had something that he felt I should hear from him. He spoke of his wife passing away but reminded me of how they had a cabin in the Upper Peninsula of Michigan that they sold a few years previously. He told the story of how he and his wife drove to the cabin and emptied it out of linens, table service, and other things. It was late in the evening and totally dark when they finished. They agreed that they'd drive until they find a motel and stay the night, then get up the next morning and finish driving back to Grand Rapids.

Harry continued his story of how they saw some pulsating lights on the driver's side of the car which had stayed parallel to them. After some time, the lights disappeared, and a few minutes later, a UFO came right up the highway in front of them, stopped, and somehow cut off the power of their car. The UFO had turned on a reddish light on the underside of it and slowly moved to the back of the car just above the roof. The UFO moved slowly, seemingly observing its occupants. The UFO then moved slowly to the front of the car, shut off its observation light, angled toward the sky, and shot off into the dark. Harry and his wife sat motionless for a short while, and then he turned the key to start the engine. All seemed well as they drove down the road without speaking to each other for many miles.

Finally, Harry spoke to his wife and asked, "Was what happened to us back there for real?" His wife answered yes.

Harry said to me that they didn't speak of the incident again or to others, but he felt compelled to tell me. Why? Time would tell.

About ten years later, I met a man in the stock department of a utility company that I worked for at the time. His name was George, a good, level-headed person. One day when I stopped by the stock department, George said "I have something that my wife and I don't speak of."

And he said he had something that he felt I should hear from him. He spoke of seeing a UFO about thirty feet above his parents' home on 10 Mile Road, on the east side of Rockford, Michigan, late at night while taking his children out to the car to go home. He dashed inside his parents' home and told his wife and parents to come out and see the UFO. By then the UFO had moved to the east end of the home and then dropped down to just above the weeds of the field next door. It traveled slowly to the tree line, angled toward the sky, and shot off into the dark.

Once again, why am I being told of this incident? Time would tell.

Years passed by, and my wife and I planned on retiring. We moved to Cedar Springs, Michigan, in the spring of 2015, and I reviewed the book once again called *Light Years.* It was simply amazing. My wife and I spent the latter half of 2015 talking from time to time about the book and Christianity. Our life seemed stifled in dogma, rituals, and many unanswered questions, even for a person with a Doctorate in Apologetics. Questions such as where did all the different races on the earth come from? Why are there discrepancies in the occurrence of the Great Flood stories from around the world? Who is actually in charge….or not….when it came to actual events where hundreds and thousands of people are killed in catastrophes, wars and illnesses? And how come Ezekiel, chapter 1, speaks of objects that are like UFO with living creatures/humans that are tethered to life tubes/lines from the UFO, yet no preacher or evangelist would dare to speak from the pulpit and claim they are UFO and aliens.

The questions were so compelling that we began to research the website http://www.theyfly.com/, which spoke of the life and times of "Billy" Eduard Meier and his contacts with aliens from the Pleiades. What was most intriguing was the fact that there was actually a book that could teach mankind peace, freedom, and harmony called the *Goblet of the Truth,* which was revealed through Billy Meier (the last of seven prophets) so that he could write it down in a complete manner. After ordering the *Goblet of the Truth,* my wife and I sat down daily and read a page at a time and discussed the many topics of life, learning, and getting along with mankind. Fantastic. No dogmas, rituals, holy days to keep, etc., etc. Just a plain and clear understanding of how to learn about the Creational Laws and Recommendations to help a person understand the universe and the spiritual growth within, and how to work with mankind in all kinds of avenues of life.

It was in February of 2016 that we decided to step out of Christianity and live for the real truth. We continued to study daily from the *Goblet of the Truth* and the contents of Billy's writings of his contact with the Plejaren people from the Pleiades. Fantastic revelations of truth about death, the life of the Spirit, the universe, the chronology of Earth, and yes, even the question that the Bible could not answer: Where did all the various races on Earth come from?

As my wife and I continued to grow in the Truth concerning the Creational Laws (the laws of science) and the Recommendations (the free choice of how to live a full and fruitful life and live in harmony with mankind), we asked ourselves, "could Christianity actually be incorrect? Are we in the box of ignorance? Why not research the subject?" And so we began!!!

The main point of this is the fact that we began to peak "outide the box." But what kept us inside the box? That is the first point of this study!

In the case of my wife and I, we were both raised in conservative Christian homes. There were no questions as to an existence of a God, it was just accepted that a God existed because it was taught in Sunday School and in the Preaching Service that "that is the truth and it must be accepted that way." So is it right...

A. that mankind accept something that a god stated was the truth and that all other scripture, manuscripts, etc. were wrong or not "God breathed"?

B. What if there were other writings that had historical content that were older than biblical accounts that proved the inaccuracy of those accounts?

This came down to the preaching and teaching from the pulpit and in Sunday school or church school where people were taught that there was no other book that was given by inspiration (telepathic communication) of the Christian God (2 Timothy 3:16, New King James Version), and that all other religions were wrong. And if you don't believe in the Christian God of the Bible, you would automatically be sent to a place called hell where a person would be in torment (John 3:16 and Matthew 25:31-46, NKJV).

There were a couple of problems, or lies, associated with the character of the Christian God, specifically in these passages.

A. If he loves the world so fully and states that he is not willing that any should perish [that is, face hell] as stated in 2 Peter 3:9 (NKJV), then proof of his lie is found in his non-action in world catastrophes, wars, accidents, etc. in places where the Christian message had not been revealed or dominated by a different belief system. This was a tragedy when the Christian God held mankind accountable for an eternal destiny in which mankind had not had the chance to hear it due to catastrophes, wars, accidents, etc. that took away that opportunity.

B. This tragedy was demonstrated in the Proverbs 21:1 (NKJV). "The king's heart is in the hand of the Lord, like the rivers of water: He turns it wherever he wishes." A major lie was revealed, and it was seen when there were major atrocities committed when nations rose up against nations. One of the biggest events that people, especially young people, failed to remember or grasp was the magnitude of the reign of Adolf Hitler, the Crusades, the Reformation, and many others where war had broken out, people cried for peace, yet the leaders of nations crushed mankind and the devastation that lasted for not only decades, but went down in history as such. Let's bring this down to more of a comprehensive understanding as we look at the bigger picture.

The text indicated that the Christian God moved the heart of world leaders the way he (God) wished to move them. If we looked at the lives that were exterminated, approximately 5,900,000, they consisted of Soviet POWs, ethnic Poles, Roma, the disabled, Jehovah's Witnesses, and gay men.[1] The big question that was asked was, "Where was the Christian

---

[1] Wikipedia, s.v. "The Holocaust," accessed October 17, 2018, https://en.wiki- pedia.org/wiki/The_Holocaust.

God who was all-knowing, all-powerful, and all-present when people were burned in the ovens of death camps, hung, shot, tortured, etc.?"

Now let's remember that the majority of those exterminated or tortured by the Nazi regime were Jews, and many were dissenting Christians. I particularly felt this impact from knowing that my DNA is directly connected to the ten northern tribes of Israel and also having an uncle in the Netherlands captured by the Nazis and taken to a prison camp. Fortunately for him, he broke out of the boxcar, jumped from it, and was taken care of for some time by a sympathetic German farmer and family while recovering from an injured leg due to his jump from the train. It was also relevant for me, and the whole context of why this was written, that my father revealed to me the horribleness and stench of war as he fought on the front lines for a portion of his tour with the army in World War II.

So where does this take our discussion? Back to the matter of who, namely a God (s), is in authority and what can that God (s) do to change things?

This question has been asked by thousands of people in years past, and you will find that the Christian Community in the world just shrugs their shoulders and says "I don't know!" They look at great things that the Judeo/Christian God has done in the Old Testament and say "Isn't our God Awesome, look at the great things He has done." After making that statement, they cuddle up to their pastor, preacher, seminary, or other collection of Christian people where they shove the topic of the "lack of God's action" into the category of "I don't know," or "God is sovereign" and completely ignore the truth that the Judeo/Christian God is not in control.

If the text, Proverbs 21:1 (NKJV), is supposedly true…. then why has it been PROVEN that it is false?

Let's look at another tragic situation known as the Crusades. The time of the Crusades was 1095 until 1291 CE.[2] The reason for Crusades was "to capture the sacred places in the Holy Land from the Muslims."[3] The

---

[2]   "Holy Wars," *BBC,* accessed October 16, 2018, http://www.bbc.co.uk/ethics/ war/ religious/holywar.shtml.

[3]   "Holy Wars."

number of wars against the Muslims amounted to nine.[4] The geometric mean estimate on the human life that was lost was 1,732,051.[5]

This is a sad story in history since both nations and armies claimed to have God on their side.

Now let's turn to the third example of questioning The Judeo/Christian God's ability, or inability, to control conflict within the Judeo/Christian camp itself…it's called the Reformation!

Some of the basics of the Reformation will only be stated because of the enormous amount of information about the movement is available. For this writing, we will focus on some of the main points that not only divided the Catholic Church but also the tragedy in lives that were lost over an immense amount of time which devastated the major portion of Europe.

The most notable point of interest is when the Reformation started, which is usually considered 1517 when Martin Luther published his 95 Theses. They were complaints that focused on criticizing the Catholic Church regarding practices of the Pope, doctrine (Theological) and items that had no foundation in the Bible.[6]

Other reformers had tried reforming the Catholic Church such as Jan Hus, Peter Waldo, John Wycliffe, Girolamo Savonarola, Zwingli, and John Calvin. The Reformation culminated in 1648 when the Thirty Years War ended. Many groups were born from the Reformation such as Lutherans, Reformed, Anglican, Anabaptist, Unitarian and others.[7]

The human toll of wars during the reformation was immense. Just in Germany, the "killing was between 25% and 40% of its entire population." [8]

And in what's called the Thirty Years' War, which occurred the last 30 years of the Reformation time frame, it is figured that a "geometric mean" count of lives lost was 5,673,870.[9]

Some questions that need to be asked are:

---

[4]   Linda Alehin, "The Crusades," accessed October 17, 2018, http://www.lord- sandladies. org/the-crusades.htm.

[5]   Wikipedia, s.v. "List of Wars and Anthropogenic Disasters by Death Toll," accessed October 17, 2018, https://en.wikipedia.org/wiki/List_of_wars_ and_anthropogenic_disasters_by_death_toll.

[6]   Wikipedia, s.v. "Reformation," accessed October 18, 2018, https://en.wikipe- dia. org/ wiki/ Reformation.

[7]   Wikipedia, s.v. "Reformation."

[8]   Wikipedia, s.v. "Reformation."

[9]   Wikipedia, s.v. "Reformation."

Would the Judeo-Christian God, who supposedly hates sin, sit and watch his children kill one another, especially when each warring faction claims the same God as their own? This confirms the irrational and delusional belief in a God that supposedly watches over his children. After all, think of the negative impact this has on unbelievers who shout out "if your God is so caring and powerful, why doesn't he do something about Christians fighting against each other?"

Were not done with this topic yet! Let's visit another scenario in which the Judeo Christian God tells his children (believers) in the Old Testament to kill all inhabitants of a city. In fact, very few so-called Christians know of the large amount of people that were killed at the hand of the Judeo-Christian God. The reason for this is that if people really comprehended in one sitting the topic of all the people that God killed in the Bible, there would be a real shake-up of who is or who isn't committed to a killing God….and hardly anyone would be left to have any faith in such a war-mongering deity. Let's look at the facts.

"There are 160 separate killing sprees in the Bible for which God is demonstrably to blame. It includes every slaughter in the old Testament, New Testaments and Apocrypha…a total of 2,821,364 deaths specifically enumerated in scripture as either directly orchestrated by God or carried out with his assistance or approval."[10]

Now that we've seen the failure of a Judeo-Christian God in a larger setting, which Christians ignore, let's look into individual experiences where a so-called "sovereign" God is supposed to have an integral part of an individual's life in which the claim that is made is God is mighty, God is awesome, God is on the throne, God is in charge of my life and God never fails. Looking at this very carefully, the claim that the Judeo-Christian God is in charge and looks after his own is often sung when the outcome of a situation is positive such as when there has been a tornado and no one has perished. Yet there have been times in natural disasters when dedicated Christians have suffered loss of life, injury and loss of family and/or friends. The person on one side of the tornado ravished street, who all survive, claim "God is great, we're all alive," while on the opposite side

---

[10]   Brian Patrick Byrne, Leon Markowitz, Jody Sieradzki, and Tai Reznik, "All the People God Kills in the Bible," *Vocativ,* April 20, 2016, https://www.vocativ. com/news/309748/ all-the-people-god-kills-in-the-bible/index.html.

of that same street a dedicated and serving family for God was killed or one or more family members were killed. With the new screams comes the question "why did my husband and daughter perish in the tornado?" "You were supposed to protect us from disasters!"

Now if you look to the book of Job, we see that God allows Satan to strike losses on Job such as the theft of his livestock, killing of his servants, the fire of God from the sky killing the sheep and servants, camels were taken away and the servants killed, and finally his sons and daughters were killed in a house from a great wind….all this to reveal the steadfastness of Job. Job 1:1-22 (NKJV).

The questions to ask here are: (1) Is this the demonstration of a loving god towards mankind? And (2) what type of God would act irrationally towards his own creation?

Going deeper in the facts we find that 2 Chronicles is the "bloodiest" in the entire book with God smiting "a thousand-thousand" Ethiopians per the request of Asa, King of Judah.[11]

Let's step back a minute and summarize the situation. The first example is of God not interfering with two groups of people that call themselves God's children…yet God does not step-in and stop such tragic losses.

The next example is of the Holocaust during WWII with the death camps, a dictator who exterminates God's children…yet no God steps-in to stop such tragic losses.

The next example is the Reformation in which internal strife amongst Christians, over doctrine and other practices, split the church and caused widespread death, famine and economic loss over vast geographical areas…. yet no God steps in to stop such tragic losses.

The question that now comes to mind is "who is this so-called God of mankind? When did he come into existence? What was he like?" What happened to him since we no longer hear of God smiting or performing acts of protection towards hundreds or thousands of people as recorded in the Bible?

People that claim any type of relationship with the Judeo- Christian God do not want to answer these questions because it is the first factor known as FEAR which holds a person from looking "outside the box" and discovering the truth. The **FEAR** that holds them from the truth has ***three aspects.***

---

[11]   Byrne, Markowitz, Sieradzki, and Reznik, "All the People God Kills in the Bible."

1. Fear of losing their salvation and being denied eternal life
2. Fear of losing God's blessing and suffering physically, mentally or materially
3. Fear of Christian peer pressure and losing friends and family

So how can this **FEAR** be removed? The answer lies in the history that the humans from the Pleiades have been revealing to Billy Meier since 1942 regarding religion, specifically the Judeo-Christian beliefs.

Now about this time in this discourse, Christians, and any other religious group that worships the Judeo-Christian God, raise a commotion and claim that the clearly authenticated presence, actions and information of humans from the Pleiades is garbage because the authenticity of the Plejarens is just "paranormal."

But what exactly is *paranormal?*. If we look at the Bible, and read about events that took place in the Old Testament or early New Testament times, we would read about many incidents where we would gasp and say "it's a miracle" instead of stating that it was "paranormal" because the Judeo-Christian mind tends to equate "paranormal" with that which is secular. Yet if we look at what is paranormal, as defined in the *Merriam-Webster Dictionary,* there is no distinction of it being just secular or religious; it really applies to both as being "not scientifically explainable."[12]

On that basis, we can look at Biblical miracles that are not scientifically explainable and state that there are at least 125 miracles, such as Emanuel (Jesus) suddenly appearing in a room, water turned into wine, Emanuel (Jesus) knowing someone's thoughts and God speaking to an individual's mind through "inspiration" or telepathic communication, (just to name a few) that are classified as paranormal. [13] These examples are what people in Biblical times would call miracles because the word *paranormal* wasn't invented until 1905.[14]

As we consider the definition of paranormal, we can look at the unexplainable events in the Bible as fitting the paranormal definition.

---

12   *Merriam-Webster,* s.v. "Paranormal," accessed October 20, 2018, https://www. merriam-webster.com/dictionary/paranormal.

13   *Bible Encyclopedia,* s.v. "Miracle," accessed October 20, 2018, https://christian- answers. net/dictionary/miracle.html.

14   *Merriam-Webster,* s.v. "Paranormal," accessed October 20, 2018, https://www. merriam- webster.com/dictionary/paranormal.

And when we consider the Billy Meier story of events, they really are as unexplainable in our lack of technology as the unexplainable events in the Bible that occurred due to unique events in nature as well as the laws of science that were or were not fully known at the time. This includes various signs and wonders in the sky that actually were manifestations of Ufological influence. This is why people refuse to look at the genuine proof and authenticity of the Billy Meier story…precisely because it appears to be beyond what mankind claims as normal and provable.

There is a tremendous amount of information authenticating Billy's interaction with those from the Pleiades and other ET But like the unbelievable events of the Bible, you have to research all the contact notes, pictures of UFO and landing sites, testimonies, witnesses, physical evidence and predictions that have come true as documented on the theyfly.com website.

If you do not take the challenge of opening your mind to the purpose and explanations of this book, your ignorance of the tangible evidence that the humans from Erra in the Pleiades have revealed about our earth, solar system, universe and the events that have led up to the present time will serve as witness to your ignorance as well as judgment on future social peace, freedom and harmony with mankind and the sustainability of the earth.

So now the removal of ignorance, i.e. the refusal to "look outside of the box' begins by explaining in simple format some initial information. Billy Meier was chosen by the Plejaren, the visitors from the Pleiades, to carry on a mission of bringing the truth of history as well as the Laws and Recommendations of life to the earth. Billy, early-on in his personal visits with Plejaren, had an enormous amount of questions. One of them was "who is this person (s) that claims to be "God (s)?"

Before we examine the term "God," we have to understand that there is as much, if not more, credibility regarding the fact that Plejaren really DO exist compared to being non-existent. The site called theyfly.com gives credible information about the visits with Billy, eyewitness accounts of their ships, their positive presence in landing sites, metal from their world and many other proofs. There are many unique situations in the Bible that would raise the eyebrows of people to the point that it could be said, with great certainty, that events such as the big wheels coming down from the sky, the smaller wheels being separated from the big wheels and the humans that wore something like a space suite being tethered to the wheels (like spacemen tethered to present day space ships, in Ezekiel, area actually true.[15] Yet Christians will dogmatically swear on their mother's grave that it has nothing to do with UFO's.

How about another example? How about Elijah being caught up by a whirlwind into the atmosphere, 2 Kings, 2:11? [16] In today's language and understanding we would say that Elijah was teleported into a UFO whose large flames that flickered were like the sound or shape of horses. Yet Christians will dogmatically swear on their mother's grave once again that it has nothing to do with UFO's.

But I would encourage you to open your mind and "look outside" the box of your religious beliefs, just like my friend Harry, a deacon for over 20 years in a Baptist Church, learned the hard way when he and his wife were in the Upper Peninsula and experienced a UFO coming up the road straight at them in the darkness of the night and stopped in front of their car, just above the roof, and scanned their car with a red light…front to back, back to front, then it took off into the night sky. From then on he couldn't defend his stand that "aliens don't exist."

When we see or come to realize credibility, it is a time to accept what seems "unbelievable" and claim it as truth!!! Within the first thirty days of my wife and I using light code at night to summon UFO we had several flash light back at us every time. And…we had three of them fly approximately 400 feet above us and one of them hovered about 10 feet off the ground, all lit up and only 300 feet from us for approximately two 10 second intervals. We saw it, we believe it, and it is a credible experience.

When previously a Christian and I was out witnessing, credibility of the Bible was based on the knowledge that the Bible and its events were seen and experienced by others in Old and New Testament times.

The same is true of UFO and experiences that people have had with them. You either accept their presence and influence as true, or they are testified by many people who have seen or experienced their presence. Let's look at a summary (**points 1 through 10 below**) of the many "infallible

---

[15]   Ezekiel 1:1-28 (NKJV).

[16]   2 Kings 2:11 (NKJV).

proofs" that are given in the Billy Meier interactions with the Plejaren from the Pleiades. [17]

1. Since 1975 and until May 29, 2018, there have been 1898 personal and 1389 telepathic contacts with Pleiadian/ Plejaren extraterrestrials and members of their Federation. The contacts are still on-going. 708 contacts are documented and available as contact reports.
2. Hundreds of photos taken of beamships and their landing tracks, among other things.
3. There exist video and super 8 footage. Film analyzed by electron microscope, laser scanning and computer functions, thermogram edge identification, Z scale contour, density and film grain inspection, processed by electron microscope, microdensitometer, infraredometer, vidicon tube, digitizer, image process computer equipment.
4. As of 2018 (May): 15 volumes (ca. 500 pages, hardcover, DINA4) of Contact Notes are available (Plejadisch-plejarische Kontaktberichte, German only!)
5. Subject matters discussed: Creation and its creations, origin of the universe, earth history, science, astronomy, spirituality, reincarnation, genetic engineering, terrestrial religions, human evolution, spiritual teachings, interplanetary space flight, galactic federation, extraterrestrial origin and visitation to Earth, telepathy, overpopulation on Earth, destruction of the environment, male-female relationships, government and military cover-ups, and many more.
6. Photographs of 5 different variations of spacecraft, from 3.5 to 7 meter, usually piloted by humans. Other spacecraft and telemeter discs are remotely controlled and have also been photographed on several occasions. There also exist huge spaceships for traveling through space. There are photographs of single or multiple objects, day and night settings, above and below horizon line.

---

[17] Eduard "Billy" A. Meier, "The Pleiadian/Plejaren Contact Case," *FIGU- Landesgruppe Canada,* accessed October 20, 2018, https://ca.figu.org/bil- ly-s-contacts.html.

7. 4 metal, 1 biological and 9 mineral and crystal sample. Metal analysis was described thoroughly in video tape format (Beamship the Metal), ft showed that the metal was made by a cold fusion process. This technology is not yet known by terrestrial metallurgy.

8. A 20 minute long sound recording of a beam-ship's whirring sound.

9. Depending on the type of beamship there could be seen 1 or 3 landing tracks. When three, they were 120 degrees apart, circular; grass was depressed in counterclockwise rotational direction, visible for months after landing occurred. Both existing and new grass were affected.

10. Witnesses: Additional to "Billy" Eduard A. Meier there exist more than 120 persons who have witnessed evidence regarding the Pleiadians/Plejaren and their beamships.

11. There are many Corroborated Prophecies and Predictions, 162 of them were from 1951 to 1958 alone!

This leads us to the credibility of a so-called "God" whom the Plejaren (those who have come from the Pleiades) can testify of what or who is meant by the term "God."

In 1975, One of Billy Meier's contact's was Semjase from the Pleiades. She explained to Billy where the name God came from. She said that "In ancient times…there were years of domination and cruelty by the Lyran leaders. The leaders were very developed, and portrayed themselves to be Gods of man. They were called Kings of Wisdom, by the word I (or J) HWH, which on Earth means GOD."[18]

This sad occurrence led to 500 years of war on Lyra and an exodus 230,000 years ago with ships and people to a planet called Erra in the Pleiades. Unfortunately, 70,000 people fled from the rule of Pelegon, an IHWH (God). Since that time, the home planets have been peaceful.

As time passed, exploration began and they found Earth and Milona where colonies were established. Once again, war broke out and Earth was identified as a place for deported warriors. At about that time, the original Planet, Lyra, went through a time of war in which 70,000 people

---

[18]   Billy Meier, "Fifth Contact Sunday 2/1675 by Semjase," accessed October 24, 2018, http:// www.futureofmankind.co.uk/Billy_Meier/The_Pleiadian/ Plej aren_Contact_Reports.

fled the IHWH (pronounced Ishwish) by the name of Pelegon, and settled on Earth. Peace and prosperity lasted for 10,000 years and ended about 40,000 years ago.

That being said, you now have your definition and some history of the term "God." But what will you do with it? You can accept it or reject it. Many people reject the truth because of the following reasons:

1. It was not what they were taught growing up
2. It was so foreign to what they thought was acceptable to believe in
3. It was not a life-changing event, such as leaving alcoholism for a god
4. It was not what their present Christian doctrinal belief said was true
5. It was not what their Christian social group approved, and you ended up as an outcast
6. It did not have the warm fuzzy effect like Christian songs did
7. It would end up causing them to be excommunicated or removed from membership
8. It would result in losing many friends
9. It would mean they would no longer have assurance of heaven

Personally, I was in the same situation as a former pastor and evangelist. Do I accept what is proclaimed the Truth, or reject it? As I studied the Billy Meier story and reviewed the many "infallible proofs," my wife and I came to the conclusion that the Billy Meier information was indeed the Infallible Truth.

Stop and think, religions around the world have always looked up and seen objects, which we now call UFO, come through the sky and down to meet man. They had no other choice but to call them a God or Gods based on the fact that these new visitors came in sophisticated machines in the sky and had technological advances that stunned the earthlings. These sky visitors are not figments of the imagination!

My wife and I have friends in our community that outright deny the existence of UFO. They say that they believe that their Christian God has made life on other planets but will not admit to the existence of UFO. I cordially invite them to go with my wife and me to summon UFO through light code but they refuse and say "the Bible is all I believe in."

Sad…they have been led to the cool-aid of poison.

The next chapter will expand further on this subject as we look into "what is truth, writings, archeological findings and proof of existence?"

CHAPTER 2

Appearance of Truth: What Are Its Writings, Archaeological Findings, and Proof of Existence

Writings

When we look at the appearance of Truth, we decide to believe it or not. We want to know if there is anything that substantiates what is claimed to be the truth such as scripts, testimonies and witnesses. We may investigate it for archeological accuracy and call for artifacts that would "date" the Truth. And of course the actual proof of existence through the collaboration of maps, pictures and other writings that would back-up the original writings.

For years in my youth I had been taught that the King James Version of the Bible is the only book to live by. The purpose of translating is to refrain from making changes that are beyond the original writings. Yet understand that some adaptation to "that" language is needed for the original writings to be understood in English words and thought.[19] This is where I submit the term and action of *transinterpretation,* of taking the original writings and cross-interpreting (writing an accurate thought) for ease of comprehension in the reader's mind.

---

[19] Gregory J. Reid, "What is the Difference Between Version and Translation?" accessed October 24, 2018, https://www.quora.com/What-is-the-difference-between-version-and-translation.

1. For years Christians have been taught that the Bible describes the Truth about creation, yet this statement is foil of holes it just doesn't hold water! Look at the different scholars that worked on the dating of Biblical Creation such as "Archbishop James Ussher, who placed it in 4,004 BCE, Isaac Newton in 4,000 BCE, Martin Luther in 3,961 BCE, the traditional Jewish date of 3,760 BCE, and the traditional Greek Orthodox date, based on the Septuagint, of 5,009 BCE."[20]

The dating of the Biblical history is also complicated by the fact that names of consecutive genealogical listings are not reliable. There are texts that skip generations because a son was not prominent or was not the first-born of the family. The individual could also be a grandson from many later generations! To confound matters even greater, there are no dates of when a person was born or died…only events in the history of a group, region, city, kingship, war or other notable event.[21]

To throw another wrench into the works, throw out the dating guess-work and use just scientific technology! If we do that, the "best estimates would be 8,000 to 10,000 BC for the time of the flood and 12,000 to 13,000 BC for the time of Adam."[22]

Consider that The King James Bible lists a genealogy going back to Adam as being about 4,000 years B.C., yet the Septuagint approximately 12,000 years B.C.[23]

2. The Bible states the account of Noah's flood, yet archeology points out there were many floods and each had its own extent of flooding the earth. This can be seen in the various layers of earth, formations and the testing of rocks, fossils and artifacts.

David R. Montgomery, Geologist and author of *The Rocks Don't Lie,* investigates Noah's Flood and finds that there are many flood stories that were regional in nature, not universal (worldwide), such as the Babylonian

---

[20] Wikipedia, s.v. "Biblical Literalist Chronology," last modified July 13, 2018, https://en.wikipedia.org/wiki/Biblical_literalist_chronology.

[21] "Biblical Old Testament Chronology," accessed October 26, 2018, http://www.accuracyingenesis.com/chronology.htm.

[22] "Biblical Old Testament Chronology."

[23] "Biblical Old Testament Chronology."

account, the Sumerian account, the Pacific Islands account, Chinese account, Mesopotamian and the Klamath Indian story in Oregon.[24]

The case for a worldwide flood was dismantled as the 20th Century lumbered along during debates amongst creationists and theologians. I remember very well the debates that went on between us high school students, some impromptu in the halls and some in the English class. Presently, as a non-Christian, I look back fifty years as a teenager, and former fundamental evangelical Christian, and think of how I dogmatically held the Bible as being without error, yet in the back of my mind I was saying to myself "there's something more to the story…things just don't seem to be adding up."

The capstone issue was the alternative explanations for the Siberian Mammoth carcasses. Eventually religious creationists and geological proponents clashed in which "…radically conservative Christians broke with those who acknowledged scientific findings and began to **ignore, selectively cherry-pick, and actively undermine** science to support their favorite literal interpretation of the Bible. Today we know them as creationists."[25]

The battle continues as aptly described in the *Washington Post* in 2016 when an article was published regarding the young world theory and the old world theory of when dinosaurs existed, whether they rode out Noah's flood or not and when the dinosaurs went extinct.[26] A creationist, known as Ken Ham sides with the "young world" theory that the planet is approximately 6,000 years old, as advertised at the "Ark Encounter" theme park in Williamston, KY.[27]

---

[24]   David R. Montgomery, *The Rocks Don't Lie* (New York: W. W. Norton and Company, 2012), 170—178.

[25]   Montgomery, *The Rocks Don't Lie,* 178.

[26]   Vicky Hallett, "Now There's a Theory that Noah Saved Dinosaurs from the Flood," *Washington Post,* December 30, 2016, https://www.washingtonpost. com/ national/health-science/now-theres-a-theory-that-dinosaurs-were-wiped-   out-in-noahs-flood/2016/12/30/92bec544-cc59-1   le6-a747-d03044780a02_   story. html?noredirect=on&utm_term=.58d2232dbed4.

[27]   Ed Mazza, "Creationist Ken Ham Gets into Weirdest Twitter Fight over Dinosaurs," *The Huffington Post,* April 1, 2001, https://www.huffingtonpost. com.au/2017/01/02/ creationist-ken-ham-gets-into-weirdest-twitter-fight- over-dinosa_a_21645613/.

However, there is a very large hole in Ken Ham's stand on how old the Earth is. A proponent of the same stand is Bodie Hodge who wrote *Dinosaurs, Dating, and the Age of the Earth.*[28]

1. The genealogies in the Bible do not add up to about 6,000 years. If he looks at, with an open mind, the "Usher Method" of chronological calculations using the Masoretic listings of genealogies, the birth date of BC is stated as 4,004. If the Septuagint listing is used, the date is 5,490. Yet if the "Patriarchal-Age Method is used, the Masoretic listing takes the date of BC to 10,842, and the Septuagint to 12,028. Noting the arguments of each "Method," there is no known answer to the dating of the earth or creation.[29]

2. Carbon 14, the most commonly used isotope for dating plants and animals, is limited in its accuracy to items less than 60,000 years old.[30] You will find people on both sides of the fence when it comes to dating rocks, bones and wood. The point to remember is the question of what can be used to date certain items cannot date other items. Gregory Weber addresses the issue in "Answers to Creationist Attacks on Carbon-14 Dating" when he points out that "radiocarbon (c_14) dating is one of the most reliable of all the radiometric dating methods."[31]

3. Yet on the other hand, radiometric dating is very accurate in dating specific geologic events. In fact, radiometric dating is a very accurate way to date the Earth.[32] Looking at modern radiometric dating, techniques have been tested and fine-tuned continually since the 1960's and has resulted in approximately forty different dating techniques, and when applied to samples

---

28 Bodie Hodge, "Dinosaurs, Dating, and the Age of the Earth," January 2, 2006, https://answersingenesis.org/dinosaurs/when-did-dinosaurs-live/ dinosaurs- dating-and-the-age-of-the-earth/.

29 "Why Disagreement on Dating the Old Testament Chronology," *Genesis Research,* accessed October 29, 2018, http://www.accuracyingenesis.com/.

30 Gregory Weber, "Answers to Creationist Attacks on Carbon 14 Dating," *Christian/ Evolution Journal* 3, no. 2 (Spring 1982): 23—29.

31 Weber, "Answers to Creationist Attacks on Carbon 14 Dating," 23—29.

32 "Q and A on Radiometric Dating," *UCSB ScienceLine,* April 3, 2012, http:// scienceline. ucsb.edu/getkey.php?key=2901.

these varying techniques are in "very close agreement on the age of the material."[33]

When Conservative fundamental believers in the Biblical God address the age of the earth and events in the history of the Old Testament, and especially the topic of Creation, they usually respond with a few of their favorite statements that they believe are concrete. They offer explanations such as the following.

1. What is in the Bible is complete, cover to cover.
2. God, himself was there and was involved in creation. He is the chief and reliable witness.

But as we look at the history of the Bible, is it really complete? Especially when there are writings that have been determined as "God inspired" and some are NOT? And who gave mankind the right to decide what books are or are not "God inspired"? The hot question is why Catholics and Protestants have different Bibles when they worship the same God?

The Old Testament of the Protestant Bible is the same as the Hebrew Bible in content, it's just that the books in the Hebrew Bible are not divided into "first", "second" or "third" of a certain book.

Catholicism holds to the books named Tobit, Judith, Wisdom of Solomon, Ecclesiasticus (Sirach), Baruch (which include the letters of Jeremiah), I and II Maccabees, and additions to Daniel and Esther. These books were included in the Septuagint, a Greek translation of a different Hebrew canon. When the Reformation came along, Protestants chose not to include these additional books because they weren't in the Hebrew Bible. The really strange part of this whole thing was how early editions of the King James Bible DID include them.[34]

Another case in point is what is called the *Lost Books of the Bible*. They are the following.

Mary, The Protevangelion, I Infancy, II Infancy, Christ and Abgarus, Nicodemus, The Apostles Creed, Laodiceans, Paul and Seneca, Paul

---

[33] Wikipedia, s.v. "Age of the Earth," last modified October 29, 2018.

[34] Elesha Coffman, "Why Are Protestant and Catholic Bibles Different?" August 8, 2008, https://www.christianitytoday.com/history/2008/august/why-are-protes- tant-and-catholic-bibles-different.html.

andThecla, I Clement, II Clement, Barnabas, Ephesians, Magnesians, Trallians, Romans, Philadelphians, Smyrnaeans, Polycarp, Philippians, I Hermas-Visions, Hermas-Commands, III Hermas-Similitudes, Letters of Herod and Pilate and the Lost Gospel According to Peter.[35]

Interestingly, these books are the works of several accepted Christian apostles and were close to the theme of the New Testament. What is puzzling is that you have "mortal men," not God, who were trying to decide whether the above works should be in the Biblical canon. The criterion at this stage was whether they were considered supplementary rather than false.[36]

A couple of other criteria that came into play in deciding whether writings were acceptable to be part of the Bible was seeing if they fit in. This was especially true when in one of the books that described Jesus's infancy, Jesus was brushed in the shoulder by another boy in one of the streets and out of anger, Jesus caused the boy to fall dead. Those around who saw it spoke out and resulted in Jesus striking them blind.[37]

Once again, why didn't God step in and sort out the situation instead of the whole matter festering into division between Christian believers? And more importantly, why didn't God step in and set the subject straight when these types of matters caused so much division between people as well as unreliability of what was authoritative Scripture?

ARCHEOLOGY

Archeological digs in and around Israel testify of Biblical places i.e. rivers, lakes, mountains and valleys, pottery, inscriptions, vessels and homes have been unearthed to show what life was like in the Old and early New Testament times. There are books, magazines, videos and maps that show where cities, ports and roads were located…but this is only part of the story and a very small part at best.

There is so much more to world history than what has been revealed in Biblical Archeology. This takes us back to the debate of "young world" or "old world" and the unreliability of the Bible in giving us a "total

---

35   William Hone, *The Lost Books of the Bible* (Gravesend: 1979).

36   Hone, *The Lost Books of the Bible,* 8—9.

37   Hone, *The Lost Books of the Bible,* 10.

picture" of Earth history. The Plejaran have given Billy Meier a basic chronology of the Earth as listed below which is by far a more complete and comprehensive documentation than any Biblical literature! In fact, if you spend time on the website, http:// www.theyfly.com/, and then click the link to Billy Meier and his contacts, there is an insurmountable amount of detailed historical information that out-paces, explains and corrects Biblical history.

THE CHRONOLOGY OF EARTH HISTORY

This chart shows important moments in Earth history based on information from the Plejaren. The Plejaren are 500 light years away from Earth and exist in another space-time configuration (dimension).[38]

Dates are only estimates to show the chronology of events.

- 22 Million B.C. The first Lyrans come to Earth and colonize.
- 387,000 B.C. 144,207 Lyrans come to Earth and settle here, forever changing the genetics of Earthman.
- 228,000 B.C. A Lyran leader named Asael leads 360,000 Lyrans to a new home in the Plejaren.
- 226,000 B.C. Asael dies and his daughter Plejara becomes ruler. The system's name was changed to "Plejara System".
- 225,000 B.C. Plejara's scout ships discover Earth, and colonies are founded here and on Mars and Malona.
- 196,000 B.C. War breaks out on Earth and its people are evacuated to the Plejaren. Forty years later Malona destroys itself and becomes the asteroid belt. Mars is thrown out of orbit and all life is gone.
- 116,000 B.C. For the past 80,000 years several small colonies have been tried by the Lyrans-mostly exiled criminals.
- 71,344 B.C. The Great Pyramids are built in Egypt, China, and South America by Lyrans.

---

[38]   Christian Frehner, e-mail to Billy Meier, November 7, 2018.

- 58,000 B.C. The Great Plan. The Plejaren build a great society on Earth that lasts for almost 10,000 years.
- 48,000 B.C. Ishwish Pelegon comes to Earth and builds a wonderful society that lasts for around 10,000 years.
- 31,000 B.C. Atlantis is founded by a man named Atlant, who comes with his people from the Barnard Star system.
- 30,500 B.C. The great city of Mu is founded by Muras, the father of Atlant's wife, Karyatide. His empire is sometimes called Lemuria.
- 30,000 B.C. The black race comes from Sirius.
- 16,000 B.C. Arus is exiled from Earth for trying to start wars. He hides out with his followers in the Beta Centauri star system.
- 13,500 B.C. Arus and his men return to Earth and settle in Hyperborea, which is the current location of Florida 13,000 B.C. The scientist Semjasa, the second in command to Arus, creates two Adams, who bear a child named Seth. This becomes the legend of **Adam and Eve.**
- 11,000 B.C. Arus II attacks the Sumerians, who flee into the mountains.
- 11,000 B.C. A group of ETs of unknown origin arrive, leby a leader named Viracocoha, who controlled the city of Tiahuanaco. His base was on an island named Mot. He provided the inhabitants of Easter Island the tools to build the strange statues there which represent him.
- 9,498 B.C. Atlantis and Mu destroy each other and ruin he planet. The air is not breathable for 50 years. All survivors are driven underground.
- 9,448 B.C. Jehovan, the third son of Arus XI, takes over the three remaining tribes left on Earth and becomes the ruler.
- 8,239 B. C. The Destroyer Comet passes closely by Earth and causes the Atlantic Ocean to part.
- **8104 B.C. The Biblical Flood.** (10,079 yrs. ago from the year it was stated in the contact report in the year 1975)
- 6,000 B.C. Venus is pulled out of its orbit around the planet Uranus by the Destroyer Comet and is in orbit around the sun.
- 5,981 B.C. The Destroyer Comet comes close to Earth, causing great destruction. It also changes the orbit of Venus.

- 5,000 B.C. Jehav, the son of Jehovan, murders his father and takes over rulership.
- 4,930 B.C. The Destroyer Comet once again passes close by Earth, causing tidal waves of destruction.
- 1,500 B.C. The Destroyer Comet passes by Earth, causing the Santorini Volcano to erupt. It also pulls Venus into its current orbit around the sun.
- 1,320 B.C. Jehav is murdered by his son, Arussem, who has two sons named Salem and Ptaah.
- 1,010 B.C. Arusseam is driven out of power by his sons and hides out under the Great Pyramid with his followers. They call themselves the Bafath.
- 32 A. D. Jmmanuel is crucified on a Y-shaped stake and survives.

Corrections were made by Christian Frehner of FIGU on November 7, 2018.

Once again we visit the statements that those who believe in a God that created the Earth would state:

1. What is in the Bible is complete, cover to cover.
2. God, himself was there and was involved in creation. He says so in the biblical Scripture and He is the chief and reliable witness.

HOWEVER….It has been shown thus far the unreliability and incompleteness in Biblical documentation to substantiate the accuracy of historical life and events of Earth. This also extends to the field of science in the sense that when scientific exploration reveals findings, science tends to "fill in" the blanks of who, what, when, where and how by interjecting what they "suppose" happened, who did it, by what means and when it occurred.

Consider the proof below that is more valid than Biblical Scripture!

Mexican Cave

There is fantastic information regarding aliens that have visited the earth in times past such as alien artifacts with engravings of aliens and spaceships that were unearthed in a Mexican Cave in September, 2017.[39]

There is also documentation of a "feathered serpent-like god in the Mayan pantheon who descended from the heavens and taught these ancient people about astronomy, architecture, and construction, among other things."[40]

The Mayans

A tomb at Palenque has a carving of Palenque, 2nd to the last ruler of the ancient Mayans, and it appeared that Pakal was controlling "an upward-facing machine with flames and smoke shooting out the back. While archeologists have claimed that this carving actually represented the tree of life or a descent into the underworld. Two leading Mayan epigraphers have stated that the inscriptions around the tomb detail an ascent into the cosmos."[41]

It was also discovered by von Daniken that "one of the glyphs on a stepped pyramid is where an inscription claims that it was a spot where the ancient gods visited from the heavens."[42]

Australia

In Australia, the Wandjina were ' "sky-beings or 'spirits from the clouds' who came down from the Milky Way during Dreamtime and created the

---

[39] Ivan, "Mysterious Artifacts with Engravings of Aliens and Spaceships Unearthed in Mexican Cave," September 2017, https://www.ancient-codc.com/myste- rious-artifacts-with-engravings-of-aliens-and-spaceships-unearthed-in-mexi- can-cave/

[40] GaiaStaff, "Were the Mayans Visited by Ancient Alien Gods?" November 5, 2017, https://www.gaia.com/article/were-the-mayans-visited-by-ancient-alien-gods.

[41] April Holloway, "Ancient Origins," July 29, 2013, https://www.ancient- origins.net/human-origins-folklore/mysterious-aboriginal-rock-art-wandji- nas-extraterrestrial-or-not-00701.

[42] Holloway, "Ancient Origins."

Earth and all its inhabitants." In addition, the stories of the Wandjina spoke of "huge mammals walking the Earth were once considered fantasy. But discoveries of animal fossils belonging to 'mega fauna' including giant mammals confirmed that these stories were accounts of real life events, passed down by generations over tens of thousands of years." [43]

West Africa

In another part of the Earth, Mali, West Africa, a tribe of people called the Dogon tell of a story that ", a race people from the Sirius system called the Nommos visited Earth thousands of years ago. The Nommos were ugly, amphibious beings that resembled mermen and mermaids. They also appear in Babylonian, Acadian, and Sumerian myths. The Egyptian Goddess Isis, who is sometimes depicted as a mermaid, is also linked with the star Sirius."[44]

The Dogon legend further states that "the Dogon lived on a planet that orbits another star in the Sirius system. They landed on Earth in an "ark" that made a spinning decent to the ground with great noise and wind. It was the Nommos that gave the Dogon the knowledge about Sirius B.[45]

Native Americans

If you heard a story from one individual, you might say "well that's just one persons' account," but when you hear it from many sources, there is credibility. If we look at many of the testimonies of various Native American tribes we note that there is a central theme that runs through all of them…namely their origination from humans elsewhere in the universe. Here are some of their brief tales.

---

[43]   Holloway, "Ancient Origins."

[44]   Lee Krystek, "The Dogon, The Nommos, and Sirius B.," accessed October 17, 2018, http://www.unmuseum.org/siriusb.htm. 1998.

[45]   Krystek, "The Dogon, The Nommos, and Sirius B."

Hopi Indians— "The peaceful Hopi people believed their ancestors came from the Pleiades and the general demeanor of Pleiadian aliens is reflected in the Hopi lifestyle."[46]

Dakota Indians—The Dakota "make reference to the same star cluster as being their ancestor's home."[47]

Cree Indians—The Cree claim that "in a time before history, their ancestors arrived from the stars in spirit form, only to become humans on Earth."[48]

Lakota Indians—The Lakota speak of "mysterious celestial beings that manifested themselves as spheres of light and would often choose particular children to follow them on a journey through space and time."[49]

Zuni Indians—The Zuni "offer one of many belief systems, if not actual experiences, related to ancestors who came from the sky, a phrasing that has since morphed into the more new age Star People reference, as opposed to Sky People."[50]

Apache Indian cave paintings also reflect alien lineage and visitation, tales of "star people/star beings visiting ancestors in flying craft and "passing on their knowledge."[51]

The testimonials of these Native American Indians speak with validity in their own right as well to our own un-knowledge and/or misunderstandings. The real question is "why is it that these stories were <u>not</u> considered factual in the first place?" The answer is because mankind makes judgments based on bias rather than correlation, collaboration and the simplicity of truth. This was brought up earlier in this writing and lies at the base of whether we believe a persons' word or not.

In particular, and quite pointedly, is the influence in which education from early years of learning affect our perception of how we view people, places, events, economics, and yes…even our scope of religion. Researchers

---

46   Steve, "NativeAmericansHaveNoFearofAliens. Here's Why,"April6,2017, https://ufoholic.com/forbidden-history/native-americans-have-no-fear-of-aliens- heres-why/.

47   Steve, "Native Americans Have No Fear of Aliens. Here's Why."

48   Steve, "Native Americans Have No Fear of Aliens. Here's Why."

49   Steve, "Native Americans Have No Fear of Aliens. Here's Why."

50   David S. Lewis, "Legends of the Star People," *Montana Pioneer,* accessed November 14, 2018, https://montanapioneer.com/legends-of-the-star-people/.

51   Lewis, "Legends of the Star People."

from all sciences tend to fill in the blanks and state things as if they were fact. Researchers need to listen to the Plejaren regarding the FACTS of our Universe and Earth! This extends to learning about visitors and inhabitants who have visited Earth thousands of years ago. When scientists looked at Mars and wondered about previous civilizations here, how Mars ended up in our solar system or the possibility of water on Mars, they could have found out through the Plejaren who told Billy Meier on February 3, 1995, that when mankind finally reaches Mars they <u>will</u> find pyramids, sculptures and gigantic monuments, the so-called Mars faces and artifacts from previous human civilizations…as well as how Mars became desolate and inhabitable. The Mars rover landed on July 4, 1997, which was more than two years after Billy Meier was told the information by Plejaran named Ptaah.[52]

The point to made here is the fact that when we are amongst "our own" there is an inherent push, however slight or emphatic, to bring the discussion to the point of "this is the way to go," or commonly known in informal conversation as "this is the way we roll."

In the case of religion, specifically the text (s) that should be followed, we find that within each family unit, but with some exceptions, that the parent (s) have a great influence on the children as to what to hold dear in the way of religious following. Why, because there is continuity in observance as well as unified peace. Those that have stepped out of adhering to a certain faith to choose a different faith are maintaining an open mind. They have begun to look "outside the box."

Native American stories of their beginnings were repeated generation after generation. Yet the Christian mindset, which I use loosely to include any religious denomination that believes in God, dismisses the historical writings of other faiths and claims "with their sword held high" that the Bible is the only and true writings from God. Once again, this is a perfect example of NOT looking outside the box rather than comparing religious historical evidence that Christian Scripture is not as accurate or complete as pastors, priests, evangelists and teachers in Bible colleges, seminaries and churches proclaim that it is.

I remember the lessons that were given in the World History class at the Bible College I attended right out of high school. When it came to

---

[52]   Billy Meier, "Contact Report 251," *They Fly,* February 3, 1995, http://www. theyfly.com/.

the history of Mesopotamia and Sumerian life, the history of how the gods that descended from heaven and reigned for thousands of years were treated as folklore or as myths. Now I will give them some slack on that matter since the internet was not in existence at that time and therefore the compilation of UFOlogy was not as available as today, but Christian institutions need to begin looking outside the box and understanding that the written account of Sumerian kings are not only older than the Old Testament Scripture, by thousands of years, but is just as verifiable as the Scriptural texts.

Earlier cultures and religious texts were woven into the Bible in themes and stories. "The earliest known version of The Epic of Gilgamesh transcribed during the Third Dynasty of Ur somewhere between 2150 and 2000 BCE. The earliest Akkadian versions of the story have been dated somewhere around the eighteenth or seventeenth century BCE, and were written on 12 clay tablets using cuneiform script. The standard Akkadian version that is used for a majority of the current translations was found in the library of Ashurbanipal in Nineveh, and was written between 1300 and 1000 BCE. The theoretical date that religious scholars believe that the Hebrew Bible, the Torah was written by Moses is between 1446 and 1406 BCE. Just by those dates alone, it shows that The Epic of Gilgamesh was written a minimum of 500 years before Moses first wrote the first books of the Torah. Also, you will find that even in the book of Ezekiel, which was written around 550 BCE, there are references to Sumerian deities. In Ezekiel 8:14 (KJV), you will find that Ezekiel sees the women of Israel weeping for Tammuz, a Sumerian goddess, because of a drought."[53]

Now we examine the historical and factual dating of the Sumerian tablets that far outpace the Old Testament writings.

"The first fragment of this rare and unique text, a 4,000-year- old cuneiform tablet, was found in the early 1900s by German- American scholar Hermann Hilprecht at the site of ancient Nippur and published in 1906. Since Hilprecht's discovery, at least 18 other exemplars of the king's list have been found, most of them dating from the second half of the Isin dynasty (c. 2017-1794 BCE.). No two of these documents are identical. However, there is enough common material in all versions of the

---

[53] Vizzle, "Ancient Sumerian Literature and the Bible," March 17, 2011, http:// www. abovetopsecret.com/forum/thread676129/pg 1.

list to make it clear that they are derived from a single, "ideal" account of Sumerian history."[54]

This is further proven at Nippur, a Sumerian city where large temples were built along with government buildings and businesses. Sumerian history and advancement was so great that there has been "found over 40,000 inscribed clay Sumerian and Akkadian tablets of epic tales such as the Creation story, legal documents, medical records and school texts."[55]

When we look at manuscripts that support the documentation of the New and Old Testaments, we find that in the **New Testament** there are "5,800 complete or fragmented Greek manuscripts catalogued, 10,000 Latin Manuscripts and 9,300 manuscripts in other ancient languages."[56] **Old Testament Manuscripts** discovered "in Cairo came to 10,000 and the Dead Sea Scrolls 200."[57]

The number one question that should come to mind is "Why is the Old and New Testament claimed to be true yet in the history of Samaria, that is cataloged using the 40,000 clay tablets of people and events, believed to be myths?" You can look back at Biblical events as well as Sumerian events and both have some strange information…even unbelievable events! But it is no reason to throw out the accurate and detailed Sumerian accounts just because they sound different or outlandish to the Christian mind.

The answer lies in Established Christian teachings that if people and events do not fit Biblical history….then anything else is considered false or at best fairy tales.

But wait; there are historical reports that not only go back hundreds of years…but thousands of years! They're called the Plejaran Contact Reports. These reports were transmitted or conveyed to Billy Meier through personal and telepathic means beginning in the fall of 1942. These telepathic communications were no different than what the Bible

---

[54] April Holloway, "The Sumerian King List Still Puzzles Historians After More Than a Century of Research," *Ancient Origins,* accessed November 16, 2018, https://www.ancient-origins.net/myths-legends-asia/sumerian-king-list-still-puzzles-historians-after-more-century-research-001287.

[55] Alex Whitaker, "Nippur (Sumerian City)," *Ancient- Wisdom,* accessed November 16, 2018, http://www.ancient-wisdom.com.

[56] Wikipedia, s.v. "Biblical Manuscript," accessed November 16, 2018, https:// en.wikipedia.org/wiki/Biblical_manuscript.

[57] Wikipedia, s.v. "List of Hebrew Bible Manuscripts," accessed November 16, 2018, https://en.wikipedia.org/wiki/List_of_Hebrew_Bible_manuscripts.

states about the Judeo-Christian God speaking to man by "inspiration," II Timothy 3:16,[58] or in other words by mental telepathy. The reason I mention the correlation here is because religionists are not use to the word "mental telepathy" being compared to the word "inspiration." As soon as mental telepathy is mentioned the religionists cringe due to its known association with UFOlogy.

Billy Meier was born February 3, 1937, as Eduard Albert Meier. He later acquired a nickname of Billy. The first letters of these four names spelled B-E-A-M.

From the fall of 1942 until now, Billy Meier has been taught by several humans from the DERN Universe, which is the universe that planet Earth and all other planets, suns, and celestial bodies are in, and also those from the DAL Universe which is a parallel universe in time and space to our universe.

Billy Meier was chosen as the seventh and last prophet to bring the "written" revelations of what is known as the *Goblet of the Truth*. It reveals the truths of man's relationship with the Creational Laws and the Recommendations, the recommended and free choice of preserving creation as well as the interaction of mankind with all of life through love, peace, joy and freedom. The Creational Laws and Recommendations are clothed in mankind's education, rationality, and logic that are bound in personal responsibility and the law of Cause and Effect.

Though the Contact Reports, found on the website http:// www.theyfly.com/, are not referred to as scripture or religious writings, they are nonetheless of higher and more reliable content than any religious writings because they span millions of years, testify of their accuracy by humans from the Pleiades and other constellations, events on earth and in our solar system that have been proven to be true through space programs, artifacts given to Billy (4 metal, 1 biological and 9 mineral and crystal samples proven to not exist on earth),[59] by his main instructors from the Pleiades. There are also pictures of the Plejaren ships and landing sites, over 120 witnesses that have seen the Plejaren ships,[60] heard and recorded the sound of them, and several hundred

---

[58] 2 Timothy 3:16 (NKJV).

[59] Eduard "Billy" A Meier, "The Pleiadian/Plejaren Contact Case," *FIGU- Landesgruppe Canada,* accessed November 17, 2018, https://ca/fogi/prg/bil- ly-s-contacts.html.

[60] Meier, "The Pleiadian/Plejaren Contact Case."

collaborations of predictions by Billy Meier and the Plejarens that have come true including 162 prophecies and predictions from 1951 to 1958,[61] and 309 since then.[62] We also have to keep in mind that the Plejaren are "3,500 years ahead of us in technology"[63] and know millions of years of history."[64]

Proof of Existence

Proof of the existence of older civilizations and the dating of Earth is often challenged by Christianity. It's called young earth vs old earth. Carbon-14 dating is good for dating back roughly to 60,000 years.[65] Through proper radiometric dating, which is highly accurate due to using many isotopic systems, the age of a rock can be determined going back several million and billions of years.

Without going into a lab and using all the expensive equipment, let it suffice that we look at a highly qualified scientist that is a Christian but does not hold the same views about Radiometric dating as ICR, Institute for Creation Research. ICR lays their premise on stating that the radiometric dating is flawed because of anomalies in certain situations and therefore is unreliable in proving an "old earth" perspective of dating objects.[66]

ICR cites the following as proof that radiometric dating is unreliable.[67]

- First, rocks of known age always show vastly inflated radioisotope "ages.

---

[61] Eduard A. Meier, "Predictions and Prophecies 1951 through 1958, Revised Translation," *They Fly,* January 25, 2015, http://www.theyfly.com/ prophecies-predictions.

[62] Eduard A. Meier, "Corroboration and Evidence," September 16, 1975, to March 24, 2015.

[63] Maurice Osborn, "Essence of the Notes," accessed November 27, 2018, http:// www.academia.edu/22378468/ESSENCE_of_the_NOTES.

[64] Kate Bergheim, "The Human History on Earth: What Billy Meier Was Told by the Extraterrestrials," September 5, 2012, http://www.meiersaken.info/terres- trial_humans.html.

[65] David H. Bailey, "How Reliable Are Geologic Dates?" November 10, 2018, http://www.sciencemeetsreligion.org/evolution/reliability.php.

[66] Dr. Jake Hebert, "Radiometric Dating," Institute for Creation Research, 2018, https:// www.icr.org/creation-radiometric.

[67] Hebert, "Radiometric Dating."

- Second, various radioisotope methods or even various attempts using the same method yield discordant ages more often than concordant ages.
- Third, many dating methods that don't involve radioisotopes—such as helium diffusion, erosion, and magnetic field decay, and original tissue fossils—conflict with radioisotope ages by showing much younger apparent ages.

Answers to the above irresponsible and unrealistic claims of the Institute for Creation Research are as follows.[68]

1. Dating techniques must be correct
2. The latest high-tech equipment
3. Technical details of statistical reliability
4. Contents of rock that produce an "anomaly" may not allow accuracy
5. Contamination of samples
6. Laboratory errors
7. Unrecognized geologic factors
8. Misapplication of the techniques
9. Checking through a "design age study"
10. Testing repetition
11. Age measurements on several samples from the same rock unit
12. Different dating methods on the same rock

So when we look at the "Proof of Existence," we can rely on various dating methods of items if correctly understood, applied and checked, to support the factual existence of an "old world" approach to life in the past. This is particularly true as claimed by Dr. Roger C. Wiens, a Conservative Christian with a PhD in Physics and a minor in Geology, who gives an astounding response to the "Evidence for an Ancient Earth."[69]

Also in support of an "old world" approach to dating items with Radiometric Dating is G. Brent Dalrymple who staunchly states that there is no evidence whatsoever to support the Creationist approach that

---

[68]   David H. Bailey, "How Reliable Are Geologic Dates?" November 10, 2018, http://www. sciencemeetsreligion.org/evolution/reliability.php.

[69]   Dr. Roger Wiens, "Evidence For an Ancient Earth, Radiometric Dating," accessed November 27, 2018, http://www.asa3.org/ASA/resources/Wiens. html.

the "earth is only 6,000 to 10,000 years old" and that a few examples of incorrect radiometric ages invalidate all the results of radiometric dating, but such a conclusion is illogical. Even things that work well do not work well all of the time and under all circumstances.[70]

Moving forward regarding the topic of Proof of Existence, let's look at three sources that claim a proof of existence to back up their reliability in being "stuck in the box of ignorance" or learning to look "outside the box of religiosity."

EVIDENCE: DOCUMENTATION & COMPARISON

The Biblical Account

In this section, three specific writings will be compared. The comparison will be based on the date of writing, scope of information and authentication. The writings to be compared are the Bible, The Sumerian King's List and the *Goblet of the Truth/Contact* notes furnished by Eduard (Billy) A. Meier.

The first writings to be examined are the compilation of writings called the Bible. What we want to focus on first is "when was it written, by whom and why? The second question is where does its credibility come from and why? The reliance on it is touted as substantial, yet its reliability is fundamentally questioned.

The earliest writings of the Bible began with Moses as he wrote the Pentateuch, which are the first five books of the Bible. The only possible exception was the book of Job since the authorship, language, texts and Rabbinic tradition point to the author as being Moses, yet scholars generally agree it was written between the 7th and 4th centuries BC...with most in agreement with the 6th century BC.[71] An example of the complexity of dating Job is given in the Believer's Bible Commentary

---

[70]   G. Brent Dalrymple, "Radiometric Dating Does Work!," NCSE, accessed November 27, 2018, https://ncse.com/library-resource/radiometric-dating- does-work.

[71]   Wikipedia, s.v. "Book of Job," accessed December 2018, https://en.wikipedia. org/wiki/Book_of_Job.

where it is proposed that there is a wide belief that Job lived during the Patriarchal era (c.2100-1900 B.C.).[72]

A strong argument for the dating of Job is expressed in points 1 through 3 and ending in the small comment after point 3.[73]

1. After the flood and long before Moses_ (after 2350 BC and before 1750 BC)
    a. Eliphaz refers to the flood as being in the past in Job 22:16
    b. Job sacrifices to God as head of his family (a practice of patriarchal times that stopped with Moses) Job 1:5
    c. Job's daughters received an inheritance along with his sons Job 42:15 a patriarchal practice that also stopped with Moses
    d. Job's wealth is determined by flocks rather than money that is also consistent with patriarchal times Job 1:3, 42:12
    e. The *kesitah* or piece of money mentioned belongs to patriarchal time
    f. The musical instruments (organ, harp, and timbrel) are the instruments of early Genesis
    g. Job lived long enough to birth two families of ten children and raise them to adulthood then lived another 140 years. He lived at least 200 years and possibly longer. This is consistent with the ages of patriarchs prior to Abraham. (Eric Lyons, M. Min.)

2. Job lived after Joseph.but before Moses (after 1650 BC and before 1500 BC).

    The reasoning for this time placement is that he must have lived between truly righteous men but not when other righteous patriarchs were alive. Therefore, he is placed between Joseph and Moses. Job 1:8 (Read more at wiki answers, https://www.answers.com/.)

3. Job lived during Moses' lifetime.

---

[72] William MacDonald, *Believer's Bible Commentary*, ed. Art Farstad (Nashville: Thomas Nelson, 1995), 514—515.

[73] Various authors, "Job Is Not on the Amazing Bible Timeline with World History. Why?" accessed December 3, 2018, https://amazingbibletimeline. com/blog/j ob-bible-timeline/.

Job is an associate of Moses' father-in-law. According to this opinion, Moses authored the Book of Job. Some say he was one of Pharaoh's advisors, together with Jethro and Balaam. (More on this from <u>Rabbi Buchwald)</u>

Another problem with biblical dating is the writing and authorship of the Pentateuch. They are expressed as follows.

"Development of the Torah began by around 600 BCE when previously **unconnected** material began to be drawn together; by around 400 BCE these books, the fore-runners of the Torah, had reached their modern form and began to be recognized as complete, unchangeable, and sacred; and by around 200 BCE the five books were accepted as the first section of the Jewish canon It seems that the tradition of Mosaic authorship began with Deuteronomy, which scholars generally agree was composed in Jerusalem during the reform program of King Josiah in the late 7th century.

There were also passages which seemed impossible for Moses to have written, notably the account of his own death and burial in the last verses of Deuteronomy.

More serious were a few passages which implied an author long after the time of Moses, such as Genesis 12:6.

Finally, there were a few passages which implied that Moses had used preexisting sources: a section of the Book of Numbers (Numbers 10:35-36) is surrounded in the Hebrew by inverted nuns (the equivalent of brackets) which the rabbis said indicated that these verses were from a separate book, the Book of Eldad and Medad.

Biblical scholars today agree almost unanimously that the Torah is the work of many authors over many centuries. A major factor in this rejection of the tradition of Mosaic authorship was the development of the documentary hypothesis, which understood the Pentateuch as a composite work made up of four "sources," or documents, compiled over centuries in a process that was not concluded until long after Moses's death. The documentary hypothesis aroused understandable opposition from traditional scholars.

Jerome and Luther and others still believed that the bulk of the Pentateuch was by Moses.

By the late 19th century, scholars almost universally accepted that the Book of Deuteronomy dated not from the time of Moses but from the 7th century BCE, and that the Pentateuch as a whole had been compiled by unknown editors from various originally distinct source documents.[74]

"The documentation and authenticity of the Bible is filled with problems as in dating events, people, and the interpretation of them. This can readily be seen in the research of time lines, Adam and Eve, genealogies, dating methods, evolution, Jabal, Jubal and Tubal, Cain, the curse of Ham, the descendants of Shem, Ham and Japheth, the tower of Babel, the patriarchs Abraham and his relatives, the patriarchs Isaac and Jacob, the exodus, Moses, late authorship (not Mosaic), Mosaic Law (borrowed from other Ancient law codes), special numbers and archeology."[75]

This is no more evident than in the place where it is being taught, that is to say churches of all various denominations including non-Chris- tians that believe in the same God and basic tenants of the Bible.

It is a confusing rash of beliefs that differ and cause strife and splits between church and parishioner, Bible school and student, mission agencies and missionaries. Having lived in Salt Lake City for 6.5 years there is a heavy emphasis by the Mormon Church, even though they use the Bible as their anchor point, which lets its parishioners know that members should not listen to Biblical rationale when approached by especially Catholic, Independent and Protestant believers. A stern warning is given by the Bishop that "you don't listen or read the Catholic/Protestant literature or conversations.… only what is taught from your own Mormon Church.

---

74   Wikipedia, s.v. "Mosaic Authorship, Torah Authorship, and the Development of the Tradition," last modified November 13, 2018, https://en.wikipedia.org/ wiki/ Mosaic_authorship.

75   Matthew Kruebbe, "Old Testament Chronological and Historical Problems," accessed December 3, 2018, https://sites.google.com/site/ investigatingchristianity/home/ otchrono.

This once again shows that there is fractured understanding and agreement about the lead book known as the Bible.

Even among denominations, especially Protestant and Independent denominations, there is sufficient disagreement regarding Biblical issues over whether to serve wine or grape juice at communion services, dress code, church politics, those allowed on the church board due to a previous divorce or a child that has gone astray and the parents are cited for a lack of parental responsibility.

Many Christians have left their church or denomination over the in-fighting of "what the Bible says, doesn't say, partially says, or is inconsistent in its teachings. Where will it end?

It's odd how the Bible is supposed to unite people, yet divides people. Some advice offered by Aaron Loy is that if you disagree with the pastor long enough, especially issues that you know the pastor may be shady on, of another view on or skips from teaching to avoid (hopefully) dissention among parishioners, you will grow uneasy, complain, and eventually walk away from associating with that church or even denomination.[76]

There are many other issues as to why people leave a church or denomination, but the core religious issues are what we want to focus on at the moment.

Some questions need to be asked at this time such as:

1. Is there a way of unity with the diversity of translation and application being so great?
2. How can there be a basis of authority when each person thinks they or their church/denomination is correct?
3. How can a God that is supposedly all-knowing have left such mixed up details, disunity in chronology, and lack of guidance of what is authoritative to people of Earth who are so imperfect?

---

[76] Aaron Loy, "Five Really Bad Reasons to Leave Your Church," last modified August 16, 2016, https://relevantmagazine.com/god/church/5-really- bad-reasons-leave-your-church.

CHAPTER 3

LACK OF KNOWLEDGE

There are millions of people in the world that have an opinion regarding the reality of UFO and their purpose for visiting the earth. By the way, this includes me until the truth was revealed to me through the Billy Meier story. Back in the 1960's there were accounts of UFO locally, state-wide, nationally and world-wide. I was just a young boy when I heard about sightings by people, even law enforcement…but no one had researched for why the sightings were becoming more prevalent.

The two that really made me shiver was about Betty and Barney Hill who were abducted in 1961 and the two men in 1973 who were abducted while fishing in the Pascagoula River, Pascagoula, Mississippi. I thought this was astounding! When will I see one?

In the early summer/late spring, on a cloudless mid-morning sky in 1974…there it was, hovering about 500 feet above our backyard in broad daylight. A call to the Grand Rapids Airport confirmed many reports from the Rockford, Michigan, area coming. When would I see one again? What is going on? What are they here for? Is there a way I can contact them? What, if anything, has UFO to do with religion (s)?

As the years rolled by and I finished my Bachelor in Business as well as a Master's in Religion with a major in Christian Education and a Doctorate in Religion with a Major in Apologetics in 1993, my questions on the subject of UFOlogy took a back seat. I began to investigate UFOlogy and its revelation and influence in the Bible in 2014 when I picked up a book called "Light Years," by Gary Kinder, about the first several years of the Billy Meier story and his conversations with the Plejarens from the Pleiades.

If Billy can make contact with them, why can't I? This question led to a whole new aspect of life. After researching that challenge, my wife and I began signaling for UFO around midnight in the summer of 2016. We had amazing success in 2016, 2017 and 2018. According to our records we have had anywhere from 60% to 90% success rate in contacting UFO with results ranging from UFO flashing back at us to flying 500 ft. above us on many occasions, to a close encounter of a UFO hovering a few feet off the ground 300 ft. from us, to a close brush with one on a hot windless muggy night that flew past me that shot a bright light at me and a cold brisk or air. I personally have spoke to them a few times (no signaling light at hand) and they have flashed a light back at me from one to six times.

I have seen ships from about 25 ft. in diameter to one that I signaled at in 2017 over the village of Orleans, Michigan, which was approximately 250 ft. in diameter. It hovered about 500 ft. above the village and released approximately 12 smaller UFO. I watched it with a niece of mine (in her 30's) for 25 minutes before they disappeared. Now we take people out with us and introduce them to "our friends on high." Their life is forever changed and they begin to "look outside the box" of religion and learn the truth about the Plejaren, history of our world, where people of other color came from (which the Bible does not explain), the non-existence of a god (s), angels, devil which they have proven by searching the universe and found no such thing as a religion on other planets. All of this is in the Contact Reports on the Billy Meier site, http://www.theyfly.com/.

Based on this, religionists and scientists need to look "outside the box" of their particular faith, laboratory, denomination, convictions, etc., and see how UFOlogy has been a part of belief systems long before Christianity…and even an integral part of the Bible!!!

UFOlogy in Various Belief Systems

What we are about to cover in this chapter is NOT mythology. If you DO NOT believe in mythology in the terms of the history of people, nations, the world and the universe and you are a religious person in the sense of Biblical people and events, then tear your Bible up and light your fireplace with it. Why? Because those that believe in Biblical history do not look at its oddities, fantastic happenings and unbelievable events as being a myth. Yet when you speak to those that are not Christian the response is that the Bible is a historical book, but full of myths. But why would they say that? It is because they were taught or came to believe in the realms of practical reasoning…or miraculous divine intervention.

Example: If a person did not know how a remote control can turn on a TV and change channels, one could say that the function of the remote control is of divine intervention through a hand-held device. Yet if the person understood how a remote control works, the myth of a "god in your hand" has been dispelled.

We also have to remember that if those from the Christian belief say that there are no mythological gods, then those that are not of the Christian belief can say that Christianity does INDEED have a mythological god and is called the triune god (trinity), or as some Christian circles believe one deity but of two personalities (God and Jesus) separate from the Spirit.

Where is all this coming from? It comes from a person's teaching of whatever religious script that the teaching (s) come from as given below.

- Formal teaching in a religious/place of worship
- Informal teaching in the home
- Recommended reading books, assignments, texts, etc.
- Peer association/talk/activities
- Counseling of various types affiliated with the belief system

With this said, we can clearly deduce that what is mythological or not mythological is based on what one accepts as what each person perceives is "the truth" which flows out from there the skewed perception of all religious activity and dogmas throughout the world.

There are many illustrations on the internet of those that lay claim that they can debunk the Bible, UFO sightings and the Billy Meier account of Plejaren meeting with him personally or via mental-telepathy. I face the same skeptics when I am confronted with questions about UFO signaling. Is it from a satellite reflection? Is it space junk burning up as it enters our atmosphere? Is it a government aircraft? And the questions go on and on. I testify of the truth, as do those that go with me, that…

- The UFO responds to specifically my light signaling code
- The UFO at times can be seen in its perfect shape via night
- vision binoculars
- The UFO responds to my energy (if in the area) of getting it to flash back by my request without my use of a light signal
- The UFO has come within 300 ft. of me for me to see all its external size and features all lit up
- The multiple times a UFO has flown over us has demonstrated, as in a DVD of the Billy Meier story, the superior technology of "blinking" out of our dimension and back into it just as the UFO hovering 300 ft. from us demonstrated several times.

There will be many who will still be skeptical, just like my deacon friend in the beginning of this book who will swear on a stack of Bibles that UFOlogy is of Satan because several years later he was confronted with one that came up the road toward he and his wife and stopped in front of his car just above the top of the car and scanned his car slowly from front to back and back to front…and then take off into the depths of the universe. Who did Harry feel comfortable in telling of his experience? Me, because I didn't bury my mind in the sand of ignorance, I looked outside the box.

What about you? Are you going to hide in your box of religiosity or just plain social denial? If you do, then you are blind to the overwhelming proof that UFO have been a part of our life on earth for thousands of years and you fail to "look outside the box." I was taught in high school and the Bible College I attended after high school graduation that Sumerian UFOlogy is just a myth. Yet I, and many others, have experienced their presence in present day living.

UFOlogy is REAL as I have expressed above, so don't close this book and bury your head in the sand of ignorance.

Let's start with a true living human being that has seen aliens, spoke to them, and received artifacts from them that have been tested and found to be true. His name is Eduard A. Meier and commonly referred to as "Billy." He was born in 1937 and began his contacts in 1942, telepathically and in person until 1953. From 1953 to 2014 there have been 1,209 personal and 1,241 telepathic contacts with Plejaren from the Pleiades. Their contact with Billy has been ongoing. Actually, their home planet, Erra, is approximately 80 light years beyond the Pleiades. Yes, I have actually seen one of their ships all lit up and hovering just off the ground 300 ft. from where I stood on the night of August 8, 2016. My wife and I have seen them fly 400 to 500 ft. overhead all lit up that same summer. This is confirmed in Semjase's conversation with Billy Meier at which time she states that there are thousands of humans who have visibly observed ET aircraft and still continue such contact because of people's attentiveness to sky watching.[77]

Friends and relatives have gone out with my wife and I and have seen them flash their light back at us as if to say "hello." The UFO were more responsive the summer of 2018 in their signaling back at us which I believe is due to them being able to sense our energy and trusting us more since we began UFO signaling in 2016.

All that is fine and well, but what about history, I mean history going further back such as in the 1300's through the 1700's as seen in many oil paintings at which time the word UFO hadn't been invented yet. This subject will be examined later in this writing. Surely, if many people that have gone signaling for UFO with my wife and I have seen them, then it is a positive testimony that they exist. In fact, I have a picture of a UFO that was flying overhead that I took one night in 2016.

Getting the Big Picture

A present day fact that UFO exist can be found in an organization called MUFON (https://www.mufon.com/), which accumulated the statistics of how many UFO sightings occurred in each country, each state in the United States, the shape of UFO that have been seen close enough to determine a shape, the distance from which a UFO was sighted, the number of UFO that were hovering, landed and took off, and whether any entities were observed.

An example can be given from the month of August, 2018, in which 734 were seen around the world. 464 of those sightings were in the United

---

[77]   Billy Meier, "Contact Report 039," *They Fly*, December 3, 1975, http://www. theyfly.com/.

States. The United States list is broken down further per state i.e. Texas = 40, California = 36, Florida = 3, and so on through all the states.[78]

While statistics keep the griddle hot regarding the present-day appearances of them, a few more questions need to be answered. They are…

- Does UFOlogy somehow figure into the Bible?
- Does the UFOlogical background of the Sumerians intertwine in Biblical history?
- Does UFOlogy history tie into the history of Christendom in the "Arts"?

When I give presentations on UFOlogy and the Billy Meier story, I begin with showing the presence of UFO etchings, rock art and testimonies of how their alien ancestors brought them to the geographical place they inhabit.

One of the hottest parts of the presentation, and truthfully the most quiet, is when I show the slides of art work, oil, chalk, etc., on canvas or paper that illustrate very clearly the presence of UFO. Out of those in a room that seats 50 people, there are about 2 or 3 that are not associated with a religious organization of any type. My question to the remaining religious attendees is "have you ever seen these drawings or paintings from the 1300's, 1400's, 1600's and 1700's in your church, synagogue, hall, etc.?"

The paintings and drawings that I am referring to are ones (and some may have seen them on the TV program Ancient Aliens) that show the crucifix, baptism of Christ, Moses receiving the Ten Commandments and Mary with the Christ-child.[79] A clearer picture of UFO at the baptism Jesus is shown at an additional website.[80] An additional painting of "The

---

[78]   "Stats Updates," MUFON, accessed December 4, 2018, https://www.mufon. com/stats-updates.html.

[79]   "In Religious Art," *The UFO Times,* accessed December 4, 2018, https://www. theufotimes.com/contents/News_1 1%20.html.

[80]   "UFO 'Baptizes' Jesus Christ in Eighteenth Century Painting," *Futurism-Media,* accessed December 4, 2018, https://futurism.media/ ufo-baptizes-jesus-christ-in-18th-century-painting.

Annunciation with Saint Emidius" from the late 1400's is astonishing as a UFO is clearly pictured.[81]

My next question to the group that I am presenting this information to is this. "Have you ever seen these paintings exhibited in your place of worship regardless of what your denomination or independent organizational affiliation is?" The room is silent….not a single hand is raised!!!!

I ask again. "Has your religious leader ever mentioned these paintings before in your worship service or any other religious teaching application?" The room is silent…not a single hand is raised!!!!

Why is this so? Because of the stoic teachings of the Christian community, and meaning this in a broad sense to cover any religious group that centers their belief system on God, a Savior or holy Spirit in some unified or split way, and stating that UFOlogy doesn't fit in the Bible.

Let's turn to Ezekiel chapter one. This chapter has UFOlogy indicated right from the beginning. You have to remember that in Ezekiel's day the word UFO had not been invented. Their concept of fascinating happenings that they heard, seen and experienced was based on a very limited scope of their description…so let's give them some credit for describing some things as "they saw it." [82]

My words will fall on deaf ears due to various organizations and individuals' close-mindedness, but I will attempt to at least inform them that the treasure chest of present day UFOlogy has all ready been opened up. The question is whether you want to experience this wealth of information. Remember, I was a died-in-the-wool conservative Christian, but when I saw a UFO in broad daylight in 1974, about 400-500 ft. or so above my back yard, my thinking began to change, ft wasn't until 2016 that I had believed in the Truth, the real Truth (which is not the Bible) from Billy Meier in Switzerland that was documented initially in the book "Light Years," that I realized that the UFO story is true, active, and is a part of the UFO story that continues to this day and on into the future.

Remember…! had been in the pastorate in a couple of churches and served as a campground preacher. I hold a Doctorate in Apologetics and was a staunch defender of Biblical doctrine. What is contained in the Bible

---

[81]   Diego Coughi, "UFOs in Christian Art," *Fringepop 321,* accessed December 4, 2018, https://www.fringepop321.com/ufos-in-christian-art.htm.

[82]   Ezekiel 1:1-28 (NKJV).

that helps mankind is good and well, but the foundational stones of the Bible are built on a human that called himself God….and I will write of that shortly in the coming pages of this book.

The problem with getting people to accept the truth is getting them to look at it with a non-prejudicial viewpoint…then examine how the pieces fit in. Christians, and others in a belief system, tend to process new information this way because they close their mind to the equation of reality.

Various terms such as paranormal (covered previously in this book) frightens people and they back away without checking the topic out. Another term that frightens people is the word UFO because it incites visions of people of different sizes, types, color and planet of origin which in turn makes people such as close-minded Christians and those of other religious beliefs shy away and say "that sounds weird," or "that's scary," or "there is no proof" and they become a stumbling block to their higher education in the sciences. The blatant responses by pastors, evangelists, etc. are focused around the responses of "that's just impossible," or "that's crazy."

Organizations, such as the "Trinity Foundation," stifle, suffocate and misguide people into a cult by claiming various things in UFOlogy are not true. Allow me to point out a few examples that are on their website,[83] and then follow-up with the corrections needed.

1. Claim:… "there has never been a radar detection of a UFO." FALSE: Read the following accounts of UFO being tracked on radar. (Many others are listed but not noted here).
   Oct 14, 1979—…that **U.EO.'s had been tracked on radar** at Washington National Airport, the second such incident in a week..,[84]
   August 2, 1965 of a **UFO** being **tracked** on **radar** and streaking toward Texas from Oklahoma.[85]

---

[83] W. Gary Crampton, TED, "Are UFOs Biblical?" *The Trinity Foundation,* accessed December 5, 2018.

[84] Wikipedia, s.v. "1952 Washington, DC, UFO Incident," accessed December 5, 2018, https://en.wikipedia.org/wiki/19 52_Washington,_D.C._UFO_incident.

[85] Dr. J. Hynek. "Sherman 1965," accessed December 5, 2018, http://roswell- books.com/museum/?page_id=657.

2. SETI…SETI, as you will note on its website, is 1) a contractor of NASA and cannot be trusted. It has cut out UFO film footage from U.S. astronauts several times and 2) they do not use light code like I and many others have done who have received visual sightings of UFO.

3. Abduction or close encounters as hoaxes? This is totally false. Do your homework, Trinity Foundation, and contact Peter Khoury of Australia,[86] Travis Walton,[87] and many others who have testified of the reality of advanced human life that have come to our Earth, including my testimony herein.

This said, it would be well worth time and effort to leave negative claims and move onto positive research and development.

What I had to say to them was "Get your head out of the sand, and come to my house between Memorial Day weekend and Labor Day weekend (sometimes later than that depending on the temperature and fall weather systems), and on a clear night we'll go out and signal for UFO so you can see them for yourselves.

The cutting edge of this book though is showing readers how the Bible is beyond a shadow of a doubt woven into the Sumerian history of gods in coming to earth and setting up and developing civilization. The REALITY of it in turn is tied into a more correct and detailed history of earth through the factual and detailed history of the humans, called Plejaren, and activity on planet Earth for thousands and thousands of years.

Yes, and I will also show how the "Noah's Ark" flood came into play with the Sumerians as shown by the Plejaren detailed record of the Destroyer Comet's affect on Earth to cause such a flood.

So, put your Bible down for now, open your mind and follow along.

When science investigates a matter, there are many questions to ask. One of them is what has been explored before? Another one is what is the precedent for this research i.e. is there certain laws of nature that have been tested with this research and what have the outcomes been? What

---

[86] Bill Chalker, "The World s First DNA PCR Investigation of Biological Evidence From an Alien Abduction," accessed December 5, 2018, https://www.bibliote- capleyades.net/ciencia/ciencia_tuathadedanaan06.htm.

[87] Travis Walton, "An Ordinary Day," accessed December 5, 2018, http://www. travis-walton.com/ ordinary. htmL

methodology should be followed? Is there a new approach that should be applied for this testing? And how should it be done? Am I keeping my options open to new outcomes that I can't explain?

These questions will be used to give some guidance as I show how the Sumerian and Biblical records are tied to each other.

GETTING THE LINK DEFINED
The Plejaren (Advanced Humans) Revelation

Do you remember the time that you first heard of the authorized writings of the history of your particular belief system such as the Bible, for the Christian, or Quran, for the Muslim? You probably thought that it was simply amazing…and truly they are as far as they are presented. But there is much more to the story.

What is presented next in looking at Chronology, especially as it pertains to Abraham and events prior to Abraham, is the more complete, and in some cases corrected version, based on newly revealed texts since 1942.

When one thinks of experts there is usually an expectation of highly educated scientists that have Master's and Doctorates in the areas of Archeology, Geology, Astronomy, Physics, etc., that also have untold experience and in-depth insight into the subject at hand. We, as humankind on earth, tend to rely on scientists with earthly attributes of education and experience. And, if there is something that needs fixing, we contact people that have more knowledge and experience than we do who know the ins-and-outs of the matter at hand and put their skills to the test and amaze us of what can be done.

We also know that items that have been invented for NASA for space travel are beyond our comprehension and we basically say WOW over it and it enlightens us…though we really don't know what planning, work, ideas, testing, failures, retesting, redesign, etc. go into it. Certain things are not disclosed to us at that moment, but once again we are amazed at what is invented by way of manned rockets with supplies, testing equipment and new means of sampling, analysis and observation.

Based on this, wouldn't you like to know the what, how, wherefore and how-come of the past and present that scientists do not know? The time has come but the revelation of it has been hard because mankind lives "inside the box" of only what mankind here and now has been told.

The telescope one day became the authority for revealing images of outer space. They were marvelous! But common mankind had to open itself up to what was revealed by the telescope. No one said that the telescope was an apparition or a figment of one's mind because it revealed things that were simple to see through the telescope. The telescope became an authority in its own right and accepted as credible because it revealed things that were questioned, guessed at or flat-out rejected i.e. the craters on the Moon, the rings of Saturn and the ice caps on Mars.

In 1942, Billy Meier from Switzerland was contacted by what we earthlings call an alien, or extraterrestrial. The extraterrestrial people, called Plejaren from the planet Erra, which is 80 light years beyond the Pleiades, chose Billy for the mission because "You (Billy) have already found the truth many thousands, indeed millions of years ago within other personalities and assimilated the knowledge. This is why you stand out from the great masses of human beings on Earth, and this is our reason for choosing you."[88] The knowledge spoken here is meaning the Creational Laws and Recommendations as Billy years later wrote down on paper and compiled it in book form called the *Goblet of the Truth.*

Billy is like the telescope, a foreign approach to learning the history of the earth and the universe, yet if you avail yourself to the technology of what the Plejaren have stated to Billy, you will begin to understand the immense history of the earth and universe going back millions of years. After all, the Plejaren can live to approximately 1,000 years.[89]

There are several accounts of the history of mankind and they will be explained further if you resolve to read with an open mind and NOT treat the Plejaren contacts made to Billy as fiction. You believe in scientists, doctors, and other professional findings from these type of people as reliable…therefore Billy's written contact reports are even more reliable as Plejaren professionals in "their own right" because of their knowledge of earth and the universe. As stated earlier in this book, they are 3,500 years more advanced than we earthlings!

---

[88]   Billy Meier, "Contact Report 001," *They Fly,* January 28, 1975, http://www. theyfly.com/.

[89]   Billy Meier, "Contact Report 004," *They Fly,* February 15, 1975, http://www. theyfly.com/.

Further references regarding the Plejaren will be addressed as "advanced humans from the Pleiades" so that we can we can get away from the paranormal vision in our mind of these human beings as weird creatures from a comic book or fiction story.

The True Account Is Told

It is proclaimed in Biblical history that all of mankind came from Adam and Eve, but we need to keep an open mind and look outside the box and understand from the advanced humans from Erra that in the universe there are many types of beings that came to Earth from other planets. There is also a corrected account of how Adam and Eve really came into existence and will be explained later. For now, let's first understand that there were several races from other planets in the universe, they are as follows.

The following was told by Ptaah, advanced human from Erra: "The first three peoples who first came to Earth were simultaneously the **RED** ones, the **BROWN** ones and the **WHITE** ones."[90]

The **VERY STRONGLY DARK** skinned—As told by Ptaah, advanced human from Erra" established themselves in that land which today is the continent of Africa, from where they then spread out further, some to Australia and New Zealand and others to various other locations."[91]

The following was told by Ptaah, advanced human from Erra: "The **YELLOW** peoples—the Chinese and the Japanese—are the youngest inhabitants of the Earth, because their appearance on this planet was only a little more than one cosmic age ago, and indeed, seemingly exactly 25,978 years ago. They came here from the planet NISSAN in the neighborhood of LASAN in the Lyra system. "[92]

The "**BLACK** race came from Sirius about 30,000 B.C.," per Billy Meier.[93]

---

[90]   Billy Meier, "Contact Report 236," *They Fly,* April 26, 1990, http://www.they- fly.com/.

[91]   Meier, "Contact Report 236."

[92]   Meier, "Contact Report 236."

[93]   Billy Meier, "The Chronology of Earth History," *They Fly,* accessed December 5, 2018, http://www.theyfly.com/.

The **"BLUISH"** race also resides on Earth.[94] This fact was also reported by Christian Frehner, a member of FIGU/Billy Meier group.[95]

As strange as all these facts of people, places and dates are, we must keep in mind that the Plejaren Advanced Humans are 3,500 years more advanced than we Earthlings and therefore know much more than we can imagine.[96]

At this time you may be asking "why should a person believe in stuff that seems so strange?" And I can respond with "this information is no more fantastic and hard to accept than the events in the Bible!!!!" For instance, it is totally unbelievable that the Christian God brought 10 plagues upon the Egyptians in Exodus chapters 7 through 11, Israel exiting Egypt in the book of Exodus and crossing the Red Sea and manna falling from the air for the Israelites to eat as told in the book of Exodus. These are just a few of them and are explainable in the realm of the laws of creation and the existence of advanced humans coming to Earth and performing what the Christian community would call *miracles* by way of their advanced scientific abilities that would make people then, and even now, be in wonder and awe.

Let me give you a *for instance* that Billy Meier and I have experienced at our respective locations, his in Switzerland and mine in Kent County Michigan. In the film called "The Billy Meier Story," there is a section in which Billy is filming a UFO in the daylight as it hovers near the top of a tree. Suddenly the UFO disappears and then a few seconds later re-appears a distance to the right at a higher altitude. No, there were <u>not</u> two UFO! It was the same UFO![97]

What transpires is that the ship leaves our dimension, and then re-enters our dimension at its own will. How this is done by the Plejaren is not explained in a contact report but can be seen in the real footage of the Billy Meier film called *The Billy Meier Story*. See citation below. I have also observed a ship "blink" out and back into view during several fly-overs and one close encounter in 2016. Upon observing this phenomenon, one would

---

[94]   Billy Meier, "Contact Report 007," *They Fly,* February 25, 1975, http://www. theyfly.com/.

[95]   Christian Frehner, "Blue People," *FIGU,* December 27, 2018.

[96]   Maurice Osborn, "Plejaren Human Beings," accessed December 7, 2018, www. oocities.org/maurice_osborn/ES04-2.htm.

[97]   Jack Gerlach and Michael Horn, *The Billy Meier Story* (Laughlin, Nevada: Reality Films, 2011), DVD.

say that it is a "miracle," yet there is no such thing as a miracle…only the laws of the universe in action! The authority regarding this topic is the *Goblet of the Truth* where it states that miracles are purely an illusion,[98] not possible,[99] and all happenings must function within the laws of nature.[100]

As you can see in the Chronology of Earth,[101] there are a lot of events transpiring that cover rather lengthy periods of time. But what we want to focus on specifically is the Hebrew and Sumerian accounts on earth and how their history is tied-in together through the verification of the Chronology of the Earth by the advanced humans from the planet Erra.

1. **Define what is meant by *a.god* or *gods:*** This topic was one of the first to be defined by the advanced human named "Semjase" as she was speaking with Billy Meier in 1975. She stated that "Man may recognize that a god can never assume the role of Creation or decide over Man's destiny," She further stated that "A God is only a governor as well as a human being who powerfully or dictatorially reigns over his fellow men."[102] This is further confirmed in the 70th contact notes of Billy Meier, from the advanced human Semjase, who stated that a human of great knowledge (governor) was also called an IHWH, (also spelled JHWH) which is the same meaning as "God."[103]

2. **Who the Hebrews actually were:** According to Contact Report#136, the Hebrews were known initially as the Hebraons, later known as the Hebrons, and were made up of "gypsies, dregs of society and outcasts who proclaimed themselves the first born people and the chosen ones," which they still hold to today.[104] They were one of three groups of people that were governed by Jehovan.[105] See the year 5,000 BC in the Chronology of Earth below.

---

[98]   Billy Meier, *The Goblet of the Truth* (Canada, FIGU 2015), 437.

[99]   Meier, *The Goblet of the Truth*, 553.

[100]   Meier, *The Goblet of the Truth*, 553.

[101]   Christian Frehner, e-mail to Billy Meier, November 7, 2018.

[102]   Billy Meier, "Contact 001," *They Fly,* January 28, 1975, http://www.theyfly. com/.

[103]   Billy Meier, "Contact 70," *They Fly,* January 6, 1977, http://www.theyfly.com/.

[104]   Billy Meier, "Contact 136," *They Fly,* October 14, 1980, http://www.theyfly. com/.

[105]   Billy Meier, "Contact 70," *They Fly,* January 6, 1977, http://www.theyfly.com/.

3. **The identity and coinciding exactness** of Sumerian, Biblical and Plejaren chronology of the Great Flood (Noah's Ark Flood) as stated by the advanced humans from Erra beyond the Pleiades.

Chronology of Earth: Dates are only estimates to show the chronology of events.[106]

- 22 Million B.C. The first Lyrans come to Earth and colonize.
- 387,000 B.C. 144,207 Lyrans come to Earth and settle here, forever changing the genetics of Earthman.
- 228,000 B.C. A Lyran leader named Asael leads 360,000 Lyrans to a new home in the Plejaren.
- 226,000 B.C. Asael dies and his daughter Plejara becomes ruler. The system's name was changed to "Plejara System".
- 225,000 B.C. Plejara's scout ships discover Earth, and col onies are founded here and on Mars and Malona.
- 196,000 B.C. War breaks out on Earth and its people are evacuated to the Plejaren. Forty years later Malona destroys itself and becomes the asteroid belt. Mars is thrown out of orbit and all life is gone.
- 116,000 B.C. For the past 80,000 years several small colonies have been tried by the Lyrans-mostly exiled criminals.
- 71,344 B.C. The Great Pyramids are built in Egypt, China,
- and South America by Lyrans.
- 58,000 B.C. The Great Plan. The Plejaren build a greatsociety on Earth that lasts for almost 10,000 years.
- 48,000 B.C. Ishwish ("King of Wisdom") Pelegon comes toEarth and builds a wonderful society that lasts for around 10,000 years.
- 31,000 B.C. Atlantis is founded by a man named Atlant, who comes with his people from the Barnard Star system.
- 30,500 B.C. The great city of Mu is founded by Muras, thefather of Atlant's wife, Karyatide. His empire is sometimes called Lemuria.
- 30,000 B.C. The black race comes from Sirius.
- 16,000 B.C. Arus is exiled from Earth for trying to startwars. He hides out with his followers in the Beta Centauri star system.

---

[106] Christian Frehner, e-mail to Billy Meier, November 7, 2018.

- 13,500 B.C. **Arus** and his men return to Earth and settle inHyperborea, which is the current location of Florida.
- 13,000 B.C. The scientist Semjasa, the second in command to Arus, creates two Adams, who bear a child named Seth. This becomes the legend of **Adam and Eve.**
- 11,000 B.C. Arus II attacks the Sumerians, who flee intothe mountains.
- 11,000 B.C. A group of ETs of unknown origin arrive, ledby a leader named Viracocoha, who controlled the city of Tiahuanaco. His base was on an island named Mot. He provided the inhabitants of Easter Island the tools to build the strange statues there which represent him.
- 9498 B.C. **Atlantis** and **Mu** destroy each other and ruinhe planet. The air is not breathable for 50 years. All survivors are driven underground.
- **9448 B. C. Jehovan,** the third son of Arus XI, takes overthe three remaining tribes left on Earth and becomes the ruler.
- 8239 B. C. The Destroyer Comet passes closely by Earthand causes the Atlantic Ocean to part.
- **8104 B.C. The Biblical Flood.** (10,079 yrs. ago from theyear it was stated in the contact report in the year 1975)
- 6000 B.C. Venus is pulled out of its orbit around the planetUranus by the Destroyer Comet and is in orbit around the sun.
- 5981 B.C. The Destroyer Comet comes close to Earth,
- causing great destruction. It also changes the orbit ofVenus.
- 5000 B.C. Jehav, the son of Jehovan, murders his fatherand takes over rulership. (7,000 years ago from 1977 as stated in contact #70). This is made up of 2,000 yrs. from 1977 to zero A.D., and then 5,000 years from zero A.D. to 5,000 B.C.
- 4930 B.C. The Destroyer Comet once again passes close byEarth, causing tidal waves of destruction.
- 1500 B.C. The Destroyer Comet passes by Earth, causingthe Santorini Volcano to erupt. It also pulls Venus into its current orbit around the sun.
- 1320 B.C. Jehav is murdered by his son, Arussem, who hastwo sons named Salem and Ptaah.

- 1010 B.C. Arusseam is driven out of power by his sonsand hides out under the Great Pyramid with his followers. They call themselves the Bafath.
- 32 A. D. Jmmanuel is crucified on a Y-shaped stake andsurvives.

Corrections by Christian Frehner of FIGU on the 7th of November 2018.

In the attempt to show how the Hebrew, Sumerian and Biblical timelines fit into the same relationship, it has to be recognized that there a lot of "so-called" theories from various religious and scientific perspectives. In order to have a consensus of the three, there has to be a common denominator given from which dates and events going forward and backward must have a common hinge point.

The common hinge point in this writing will be what the advanced humans from Erra have given us so that we can learn to quit squabbling about chronology. What is that hinge point? **The Biblical Flood** as seen in the above chronology of earth. It's not properly titled the Biblical Flood, as the advanced humans from Erra recognize, it's the Great Flood that was caused by what is called the **Destroyer Comet,** since it affected the world.

What I run into here is the push-back from the "young world" religionists who state that the world goes back to approximately 4,000 BC, some say around 6,000 BC and some that stretch it to 10,000 or 12,000 BC. There is a lot of conjecture at this point as you can see.

This writing will prove an old world approach to the history of the world through actual recorded facts which have been revealed through scientific documentation where you don't need to squabble over carbon 14 dating or radiometric dating methods…you just set your prejudices aside and read about the research….and I find it hard to believe that no one else put these facts in alignment so an understanding can be reached!!!!

First of all, let's be clear about the fact that there have been many floods in the past; some have been more extensive than others throughout the world.[107] But the one that cracks history open is the one in 8104 BC that the advanced humans from Erra have given us on the Chronology of the Earth as seen previously. How did they know that? They have storage banks where "everything planetary is recorded in i.e. thoughts, feelings,

---

[107] David R. Montgomery, *The Rocks Don't Lie* (New York: W. W. Norton and Co., 2012), 1-257.

emotions, acts, deeds, fears, anxieties, hopes, wishes, motions and all things a human undertakes good or bad are stored as impulses."[108]

Secondly, note that the other dates on the Chronology of the Earth are estimates but will be very close in the specific dating as will be explained as this writing proceeds.

Thirdly, it will be shown that the so-called God of the Hebrews, and eventually Christian-world, was a God just as the Sumerian Gods were. It is here that specific time and facts will be presented from Sumerian and Biblical history.

EXAMINATION BEGINS: DATING OF THE FLOOD

To preface the examination, it must be understood that dating events must be anchored on solid proof of an event such as the occurrence of a comet that caused the Biblical Flood in 8104 BC. But even more than that, the comet occurring at regular intervals such as years, decades or centuries that were documented.

If religious leaders say that they can only trace back to Abraham in a chronological way and then use a tongue-in-cheek way to guess the dates of activities going further back….THIS IS TOTAL NONSENSE THAT THE RELIGIOUS COMMUNITY IS USING!!! In addition, it robs history of its identity. If Biblical history was on trial, it would be sentenced to life behind bars for the false accusation of the religious community.

I will show that the chronology of the advanced humans from Erra have provided specific proof of dating events. You don't believe that advanced humans from Etta, 80 light years beyond the Pleiades have come to Earth? Sounds like myths? Sounds paranormal? If you hold that position, then you need to throw out your Bible because it has over 125 paranormal events in it as stated previously.

With that said, let's look at the "anchor point" of the research the path to the truth.

Q: Why is 8104 BC so important?

---

[108] Billy Meier, *Talmud of Jmmanuel* (Canada: FIGU-Landesgruppe Canada, 2016), CVI.

A: This is the date of the "Noah's Ark Flood, but why? The answer is because of the devastating affect it had it had on the <u>world</u>….not just a local flood. Genesis 6:17 (KJV) states that the flood will "destroy" all flesh. The only destructive event of this magnitude was the comet that the advanced humans from Erra call the "Destroyer Comet." However, this needs clarification.

After Billy Meier had spent time with Sfath, when Billy was a child of 5years old, a new teacher from the DAL Universe took over for a few days in 1964, and one of the subjects that he was taught was the nature of the Destroyer Comet and the Deluge it caused approximately 10,000 years ago, which Asket said was an erroneous number (as was proven in the Chronological History of the Earth and events that verified its occurrence). At about 9,545 BC, the Pyramids remained abandoned. Asket explained to Billy Meier that a King by the name of Sahluk, who lived approximately 300 yrs. before the Noah flood, had a son who had the ability to see the future and destruction of lives from a comet. The King ordered food preparation and storage of it in the Pyramids and underground villages which alerted future kings and people of needed preparation. The pyramids were also covered with coatings of Lime to keep the water out. [109]

So in essence, all flesh was destroyed as the Bible stated…but there was an exception due to those in hiding under the pyramids.

Q: Were there other floods?
A: Yes, Before and after 8104 BC. Just a reminder, this is NOT Halley's Comet!

The Destroyer Comet comes ever 575.5 years,[110] as the advanced humans from Erra have pro claimed and it's been consistently on time.

Lists of the dates that correspond to the Destroyer Comet are as follows along with verifications.

8104 BC 10,079 years ago from the year 1975, resulted in the rotation and tilt of the Earth being changed, hours per day changed from over

---

[109] Billy Meier, "Asket's Explanations Part 4," *They Fly,* February 9, 1953, http:// www. theyfly. com/.

[110] Billy Meier, "Contact 5," *They Fly,* February 16, 1975, http://www.theyfly. com/.

40+ to 24hr., Sun rose formerly in a different direction and the Destroyer Comet will come again every 575.5 years +-. Large storms over the ocean rose waves 2,000 meters and destroyed landscapes and harbors in Syria. Egypt floods which in turn causes epidemics.[111]

8,000 BC is an **approximate date** to the ancient civilizations of Mesopotamia and the Indus Valley.[112]

8100 BC disaster in Egypt resulted in geologic change and mass extinction.[113]

8100 BC is an **approximate** flood date for one of two Tsunami that hit the Shetland Isles called the Storegga Slide Tsunami.[114]

7528 BC Destroyer Comet came

6953 BC Destroyer Comet came

6377 BC Destroyer Comet came

5802 BC Destroyer Comet came

5226 BC Destroyer Comet came

4651 BC Destroyer Comet came

4075 BC Destroyer Comet came

3500 BC: At precisely 3453 BC, the Destroyer comet came and created catastrophic changes—large loss of life to humans and animals, shift of mountains, tearing apart of lava walls of the Santorin Volcano in the Mediterranean Sea, flooding in Egypt causing epidemics, and destruction of landscapes and harbors in Syria.[115]

3400-3100 BC: There was an emergence of society (after the flood) with laws, astronomy, agriculture, and the invention of the wheel in Egypt, Mesopotamia, and the Indus Valley.[116]

3450-3250 BC: There was an anomalous silt layered in peats on Achill Island, extreme tree growth downturned in Ireland, tree ring

---

[111] Meier, "Contact 5."

[112] Laura Lee, "Japans Mysterious Submerged Stone Structures," accessed January 5, 2019, https://www.bibliotecapleyades.net/arqueologia/esp_ruinas_yonaguni_6.htm.

[113] Carrie Kozikowski, "Geological History Recorded by Missing Ancient Civilizations," last modified December 24, 2000, http://home.hiwaay.net/^jal- ison/CARRIE2.htm.

[114] Bondevik, et al., "The Case for Significant Numbers of Extraterrestrial Impacts through the Late Holocene," *Journal of Quanternary Science* (2007): 101—109, https://doi.org/10.1002/qs. 1099.

[115] Billy Meier, "Contact 5," *They Fly*, February 16, 1975, http://www.theyfly.com/.

[116] B. Warmkessell, "Vulcan and Comets Related Sites: The 3500 BC Strike," accessed January 6, 2019, http://barry.warmkessel.eom/4related.html#cl.

chronologies that were the same from Switzerland to England along with an exceptional sulphate event in the ice core and consistent with a deposition of biogenic sulphate.[117]

2924 BC Destroyer Comet came

2349 BC Destroyer Comet came

1773 BC Destroyer Comet came

1198 BC Destroyer Comet came

622 BC Destroyer Comet came

47 BC Destroyer Comet came

528 BC Destroyer Comet came

1104 AD Destroyer Comet came February 2, **1106,** returned in **1680** after a 575 year interval[118]

1680 AD Destroyer Comet came in **1680.** Confirmed in the book *The New World: Extra Series,* ft also verified it was the same comet of AD 1104 and came every 575 years approximately.[119]

Destroyer Comet of the 1680 came November 29, **1680.**[120]

Destroyer Comet of 1680 was witnessed by Sir Isaac Newton; calculated by William Whiston to return every 575 years.[121]

From the anchor point of the Destroyer Comet of 8104 BC, the verification of its re-appearance is listed in the dates following 8104 BC. Specific dates of 8104, 3500 BC, 1104 AD and 1680 AD have been elaborated on to show that these dates were particularly note-worthy due to the devastation that occurred. These dates fall in line with the advanced human declaration of the Destroyer Comet appearing every 575.5 years.

It should be noted that the further back in time there is a loss of the documentation of the Destroyer Comet as well as other comets due to the

---

[117] Gary C. Daniels, "Did a Comet Hit Earth the Last Time the Mayan Calendar Ended?" December 2012, https:therealmayanprophecies.com/did-a-comet-hit-earth-the-last-time-the-mayan-calendar-ended/.

[118] Wikipedia, s.v. "X/1106 Cl," accessed January 7, 2019, https://en.wikipedia. org/wiki/X/1106_C 1.

[119] P. Benjamin, *TheNew World: Extra Series* (New York: J. Winchester Pub., 1842), 16, https:book.google.com/books?id=42QoAQAAMAAJ.

[120] Wikipedia, s.v. "Great Comet of 1680," accessed January 6, 2019, https:// en.wikipedia. org/wiki/Great_Comet_of_1680.

[121] Mark Strauss, "Why Newton Believed a Comet Caused Noah's Flood," *National Geographic,* December 30, 2016, https://news.nationalgeographic. com/2017/01/comet-new-years-eve-newton-flood-bible-gravity-science/.

lack of reporting and archiving of such events. Therefore, researchers in the science of comets will express a date of **approximation** due to a lack of records or dating problem and still be within a margin of error 2% or 3% from the authorized date on the list.

It should also be noted that there is no mix-up with the dates of the Destroyer Comet and Halley's Comet. The record of Halley's Comet starts June 3, 240 BC. The closest Halley's Comet has come to the Destroyer Comet dates are as follows.

Destroyer Comet date 1104 AD, Halley's Comet 1066 and 1145 AD.

Destroyer Comet date 1679 AD, Halley's Comet 1682 AD.

Halley's Comet passes Earth every 75 or 76 years, yet the Destroyer Comet passes by every 575.5 years. The Destroyer Comet discovered by Gottfried Kirch and then labeled the Kirch Comet came in 1680 AD. Halley's Comet came two years later in 1682 AD. So we have to be careful not to mix the two comets up.[122]

In previous pages we have seen the testimony of the Noah's Ark flood of 8104 BC as being specifically dated by the advanced humans from Erra. Those that have suggested the same date or estimated date around 8104 BC have not testified of the same or estimated date but have come up with their guess based on the historical occurrence of the Destroyer Comet as well as destructive data from that time period.

Geologists William Ryan and Walter Pitman of the Columbia University suggested that there was a "shift in the Earth's axis", about 10,000 BC, which resulted in the melting of ice at the poles "around 7,000 BC and the subsequent rise in the levels of the oceans and the flooding of the land.[123]

Another author/researcher basically hit it on the head by pointing out "three major geologic changes in the Earth's history" with the dates of 20,200 BC, 12,200 BC and 8,100 BC." Using the occurrence of 575.5 years for the Destroyer Comet passing by Earth, each of the dates are within 11, 68 and 4 years respectively.[124]

---

[122] Wikipedia, s.v. "Great Comet of 1680," accessed January 6, 2019, https:// en.wikipedia. org/wiki/Great_Comet_of_1680.

[123] April Holloway, "Ancient Origins," March 20, 2013, https://ancient-origins. net/human-origins-folklore/great-flood-through-sumerian-tablets-00240.

[124] Carrie Kozikowski, "Geological History Recorded by Missing Ancient Civilizations," accessed January 8, 2019, http://home.hiwaay.net/-jalison/ CARRIE2.htm.

However, another problem arises when Religionists and secular sciences state that Noah's Flood took place about 3,500 BC. Yes, there was a major flood at that time created by the Destroyer Comet…that occurrence is a fact as was shown in previous pages. But this flood was **not** as devastating as the 8,104 BC passing of the Destroyer Comet because the 8104 BC comet went even further in creating havoc by changing the Earth's rotation "from over 40 hours a day to the current 24 hours a day" as well as "changing the direction of the rising sun."[125]

Tying It Together: Identifying the *Who*

So how does the Biblical history fit into the flood of 3,500 BC and the Noah flood of 8104 BC? Many have tried it because 1) a lack of knowledge, 2) incomplete knowledge, 3) erroneous knowledge, and 4) no knowledge at all. Any one of these four options has led mankind to make some super mistakes in chronology and historical events. This is particularly important when it comes to the Biblical Scriptures where there is "no definite date for the creation of mankind" in the context of earth scientific exploration and dating other than carbon and radiometric dating where applicable and reliable.[126]

Finding pottery and artifacts give clues to certain civilizations, but the cutting edge of all this history is the reliability of boots-on-the-ground. One special source in which boots-on-the ground is particularly reliable is the humans from Erra, specifically known as the Plejaren who come from a planet just 80 light years beyond the Pleiades.

This is the big problem with Religious and scientific people who close their eyes to the reality of the history that is revealed to Billy Meier through the contact notes that Billy has recorded from conversations with the technological advanced humans from Erra. In fact, it is more reliable than the Bible, Quran, and any other religious texts because of the specific details that are given such as in the events of the earth, moon, planets, our solar system, comets, civilizations, and universe.

---

[125]   Billy Meier, "Contact 5," *They Fly,* February 16, 1975, http://www.theyfly. com/.

[126]   Dr. George E Isham, "Chronology: A Proposed Harmony Between Genesis and the Sumerian King List," last modified August 21, 2014, https://sites.google. com/site/ drgeorgefisham/system/app/pages/recentChanges.

I challenge you to check out the Billy Meier site at http://www. theyfly. com/ and use the search box in the upper right corner of the web page. It may take you awhile to acclimate yourself to the site and all the topics you can "click on" to get to the information that you seek….but keep trying and you'll begin to get comfortable on the information available. I would also suggest you start reading the "Contact Reports" under the heading of "Billy Meir Contacts" because there is some fantastic scientific information beginning with contact report #1.

I trust by now that you have checked out the "Sumerian King List." The **first topic** we want to examine is the Kingship from "heaven." This information tells us that the Kingship was real, not a ghost, spirit or apparition. They came with flying ships that "descended from heaven, meaning the heavens or that which is above the earth. They were real humans with lives that extended centuries. We shouldn't marvel at this because it is a common theme in stories, movies, etc. where the storyline involves a human or creature that has an extensive existence.

As I said earlier in this writing, you have to keep an open mind because we tend to judge what is unseen by what we see and know which means that anything outside our present comprehension is usually discarded. To understand how this history works we must challenge the unbelievable. We will see how this holds true when examining the aging of those who lived in Eridug as well as those who had longevity in the Bible.

This is not so strange if we consider the advanced humans from Erra beyond the Pleiades. The lady that was one of Billy Meier's main instructors by the name of Semjase advised him after several meetings that though she looked to be about 33 years old, she was actually 330 years old and that their life expectancy is about 1,000 years.[127]

In a later conversation that Billy had with Semjase, she told him about another human form of life on earth that died out 230,000 years ago that had an average life span of 1,500 years.[128]

In the Sumerian King List, we do not know where the humans known as "Gods" came from, but we do know that they were called "IHWH"

---

[127]   Billy Meier, "Contacts," *They Fly,* February 8, 1975, http://www.theyfly.com/.
[128]   Billy Meier, "Contact/," *They Fly,* February 25, 1975, http://www.theyfly.com/.

(sometimes spelled JHWH with the "J" pronounced as "I") which has the same meaning as "God" and meaning "Kings of Wisdom."[129]

From here we pick up the Chronology of Earth History, as revealed by the advanced humans from Erra beyond the Pleiades, to focus on the Hebrews as to who they are and how they fit into a "god-belief" system based on the "advanced humans" of Sumaria and its reflection on Abraham's belief in a so-called God which is the same as the Sumerian belief system.

From here, the reader needs to follow closely and keep an open mind because Contact #70 states that the Hebraons, later called Hebrons and finally Hebrews, were synonymous with "gypsies, dregs of society and outcast" rather than the present mindset of gypsies that are wanderers, traveling and an unsettled type of people.[130]

Identifying the *Wherefore*

Identifying the "wherefore" comes from the fact that some event follows a previous event. In this research the "wherefore" establishes a setting that goes from the worship of "Gods" to Abraham's choice of following "a" God, and others would say "thee" God. The following of a God by Abraham would change that reference due to a so-called personal relationship to a specific God.

Once again we must be reminded that there is no clear chronology of time in the Bible. The ages of people in the Bible go back to more than 900 years in some cases, but what reliable dates can be used of when these people lived? The creationists claim that the existence of man goes to about 4,000 years, yet archeology findings have identified individuals and civilizations going back thousands of years. Some of those archeology finds are as follows.

- A 400,000 year old cranium found in a Portuguese cave.[131]

---

129   Billy Meier, "Contact 70," *They Fly*, January 6, 1977, http://www.theyfly.com/.
130   Meier, "Contact 70."
131   Maria Gallucci, "This 400,000-Year-Old Cranium Offers New Clues on Human Evolution," *Maskable*, March 13, 2017, http://mashable.com/2017/03/13/human-fossil-evolution-portugal/#gj_Dom4N4EqI.

- Humans in America 100,000 Years Before We Thought?[132]
- 14,000 year old village…began in North America[133]
- Human footprints in hardened volcanic ash 3.7 million years ago.[134]
- We always knew our ancestors were microbes. Now we found them.[135]
- Strange Archaeological Discoveries…at nearly 2 million years old, it shows evidence of human-like dwellers.[136]

One of the greatest records of the history of man is "The Chronology of earth History." The record was given to Billy Meier by the advanced humans from Erra which is 80 light years beyond the Pleiades. The Chronology goes back to 22 million years BC. Contact Report#70 discusses the many events regarding the coming and going from Earth by various advanced humans, wars that took place, disasters by means of comets, the pyramids, the great cities of Atlantis and Mu, the black race coming to Earth, Easter Island and the Sumerians.

These accounts may seem strange, but they have been proven true through the records of the advanced technological humans from Erra, science, eyewitness accounts and archeological proof.

---

[132] Canida Moss, "Were Humans Really in America 100,000 Years Before We Thought?" *The Daily Beast,* April 29, 2017, http://www.thedaily- beast.com/articles/2017/04/29/ were-humans-in-america-100-000-years-before-we-thought.

[133] TimCollins, "Revealed: 14,000-Year-01dVillage '01derThan Egyptian Pyramids' Sheds Light on How Civilization Began in North America," *MailOnline,* April 10, 2017, http://www.dailymail.co.uk/sciencetech/article-4397970/14-000-year-old-village-older-pyramids-found.html#ixzz4dx9u6Y00.

[134] Malcom Ritter, "Ancient Human Ancestor Was One Tall Dude, His Footprints Say," *AP Science Writer,* December 14, 2016. His recent work can be found at http://bigstory.ap.org/content/malcolm-ritter.

[135] Sarah Kaplan, "We Always Knew Our Ancestors Were Microbes," *Washington Post,* January 12, 2017, https://www.washingtonpost.com/news/speak- ing-of-science/wp/2017/01/12/we-always-knew-our-ancestors-were-microbes- now-we-found-them/?utm_term=.0bbf73ee3ef6.

[136] Wikipedia, s.v. "Olduvai Gorge," accessed January 12, 2019, https://en.wikipe- dia.org/wiki/Olduvai_Gorge±

Identifying the *Which Is*

Moving on from the "Wherefore," the research develops into "Which is This" or "Which is That?" Religious and secular histories are smitten with questions where records do not exist, partially exist, or fully exist but questionable due to a lack of authenticity. One of the greatest sources of proven history, and historians both religious and secular need to rely on, are from the advanced humans from Erra in the Pleiades. Now as soon as I mention this source of history there is an outcry from the religious community that "their" religious text is complete and true from cover to cover. Sorry folks, this **is not true.**

A number of critics of the Bible have challenged it from various standpoints including proof of humans existing before the timeline of approximately 4,000 years BC. This filters down to kids in grade school thinking that man did not appear until 4,000 BC. Hebrew stories have been influenced in context by Sumerian literature, the error of scribes in copying down details, the Adam and Eve story as being fabricated and religionists (the "young world" group) even questioning the methods of dating of information and artifacts in the areas of geology, history, biology, astronomy and archaeology. Even the timing of the Biblical flood, the curse of Ham and the dividing of languages is purely false as explained by Matthew Kruebbe, University of Texas at Tyler (1999).[137]

Another source challenges Biblical issues such as the missing of genealogical families as they relate to the Septuagint and Masoretic Text, the timing of the Flood and gaps in genealogies.[138]

Case in point: When I was a kid and we played flag football in the street and a disagreement broke out amongst the players, one team blamed the other for a cheating move at one point or another. The next thing you know there were inappropriate words flying and a potential for fists to do the same. However, there were a couple of mothers from both teams that had been observing the game from their windows and saw the whole

---

[137] Matthew Kruebbe, "Old Testament Chronological and Historical Problems," *Investigating Christianity,* accessed January 14, 2019, https://sites.google.com/ site/ investigatingchristianity/home/otchrono.

[138] "New Perspectives Affirming the Biblical Genesis Record, the Creation Account," *Genesis Research,* accessed January 14, 2019, http://www.accuracyin- genesis.com/.

matter evolve. One mother would see it from where she stood, another mother from where she stood, which didn't put the whole thing into perspective until a third mother saw very clearly and completely from her total and clear view EXACTLY what had happened to bring such a heated exchange of players to a head.

The lady who saw the whole matter did not speak up at that moment but waited due to the hot-headedness between the players and the incomplete details of two mothers. Once a week the mothers would have a "ladies neighborhood" coffee where they would meet and talk about kids, husbands, social life and…the football game in the street a few days earlier. The ladies gave their perspective of the game as to "whose fault" resulted in harsh words back and forth until the mom who saw the whole matter, who had a birds-eye view of the whole game, spoke up and clarified who in the football game acted un-sportsman-like and cheated.

This example is likened to the genealogies and stories of Biblical events whereby no writer wrote down the complete story. I went through such questioning early in 2016 when I asked myself *Where had people of all different-colored skin come from? The* answer was provided by the advanced humans from Erra beyond the Pleiades in Contact Report 7. Why couldn't the Bible tell me that? Another error in Biblical history!

Another question that came to my mind was of course the chronology of the Biblical names, and was it the complete list?

We have seen the date of 8104 BC as being the date of the "Noah Flood," this was the most devastating flood caused by the Destroyer Comet. The comet came back in 3,453 BC and created a large amount of havoc as documented a few pages back. So we are concerned about the 8104 BC date which means that there has to be more to the story of genealogies, which there certainly is.

In the Talmud of Jmmanuel (the "J" is pronounced as "I"), there is an extensive genealogical list of people from Adam to Joseph. There is some history involving certain individuals which I will not go into due to keeping-to-the-subject of genealogy and the amount of names that should have been inserted in the original genealogical list that demonstrates Noah's Flood date of 8104 BC. The correct list of genealogies is as follows.[139]

---

[139]   Billy Meier, *Talmud of Jmmanuel* (Canada: FIGU-Landesgruppe Canada, 2016), 20-24.

"Adam, Seth, Enos, Akjbeel, Aruseak, Kenan, Mahalaleel, Urakjbarameel, Jared, Henoch, Methusalah, Lamech, Tamjel, Danel, Asael, Samsafeel, Jomjael, Turel, Hamech, Noah, Sem, Arpachsad, Batrael, Ramuel, Askeel, Amers, Salah, Eber, Peleg, Regu, Serug, Araseal, Nahor, Thara, Abram. Jsaak, Jakob, Juda, Ananj, Ertael, Perez, Hezron, Ram, Amjnadaab, Savebe, Nahesson, Sahna, Boas, Obed, Jesse, David, Salomo, Asa, Gadaeel, Josaphat, Jora, Armeneel, Usja, Jothan, Gadreel, Ahas, Jtjiskja, Manasse, Amon, Josja, Jojachjn, Sealthjel, Jegun, Serubabel, Abjud, Eljakjm, Asor, Zadok, Achjm, Eljud, Eleasar, Matthan, Jakob, Joseph."

As we continue to identify the "which is," we have to look at what information is stable or factual, and what is not. Let's review what we know and don't know in order to safely move forward in religious truth, or religious muck.

1. We know that the Biblical Scripture is factual in part, but not in whole.
2. We know that the dating of events and placement of people is incorrect due to the guessing of dates and the lack of information.
3. We know that translations of Biblical literature have been through the ringer of human error and are not reliable in transcribing or in detail.

From here, we need to establish the truth of identity in the realm of "a" God or "Gods," or identifying the "wherefore" of God and man.

Identifying the *Wherefore*

Two topics under this heading will be reviewed here, 1) who and where did the Gods that came down from heaven come from, and 2) how does that relate to the God of the Bible?

In the Sumerian King list we are told that the kingship "descended from heaven."[140] This reference is to the area which is above the atmosphere of the earth, not a place in the corner of the universe. The advanced

---

[140] Wikipedia, s.v. "Sumerian King List," accessed January 14, 2019, https:// en.wikipedia. org/wiki/Sumerian_King_List.

humans from Erra even confirmed that there is no "hell,"[141] and there is no "heaven."[142] These truths are also found in the *Goblet of the Truth* in many verses which can be accessed through the website http://www.theyfly.com/ and clicking on the "Topic Index to the *Goblet of the Truth*" then scrolling down to the topic of your choice.[143]

This whole scenario of the kingship coming to Earth should not sound odd. And once again, I remind the religionists to keep an open mind because as soon as they scream the words *myth* or *paranormal,* they need to remember that their so-called angels, demons, etc. had supposedly come down to Earth for their mythical or paranormal activities in spaceships.

Just imagine with me for a moment how those in the UFO's, off in a distant Moon Crater,[144] were saying when Buzz Aldrin and Neil Armstrong landed on the moon…. possibly "the kingship from Earth has arrived!" Yes, there are advanced human personnel in the universe. Time will tell regarding contact with them what the specifics are about their origination and their purpose.

Yes, people of advanced technology are real and had an impact on the early history of Earth. If you review the Chronology of the Earth that was pointed out earlier in this writing you will see the many "comings and goings" of activity. So why would we be so surprised if advanced humans were on the moon checking out the activities of the U.S. astronauts?

In fact, Billy Meier became acquainted with 48 individuals from the Plejaren Star system, the DAL Universe (a parallel universe to our DERN universe), the Vega Star System, the Lyra Star System, the Cygnus Star System, the Nol Star System and the Coma Galaxy.[145]

We now get back to the first question. Where did the advanced humans come from in the "Sumerian King List? That question still remains unanswered. There have been several suggestions by various individuals but they are all pure conjecture and only serve to confuse the reader.

---

[141]   Billy Meier, "Contact 6," *They Fly,* February 5, 1975, http://www.theyfly.com/.

[142]   Billy Meier, "Contact 10," *They Fly,* March 26, 1975, http://www.theyfly.com/.

[143]   Billy Meier, "Heaven and Hell," in *Goblet of the Truth* (Canada: FIGU- Landesgruppe Canada, 2015).

[144]   Gaia Staff, "What Did NASA Really Discover on the Moon During The Apollo Missions?" July 19, 2017, https://www.gaia.com/article/ what-did-nasa-really-discover-on-the-moon.

[145]   Billy Meier, *Pleiadian/Plejaren and with them Federation Contact Persons* (Canada: FIGU-Landesgruppe Canada).

What we DO know is that they were living intelligent humans, known as kings, who had the ability to live for extended life spans and leave at will, as mentioned in the Sumerian King List, just before the flood of 8104 BC and how the kingship returned after the flood. We can also see detailed historical information about various advanced humans coming and going from Earth in the Chronology of Earth History as described earlier in this work and even specifics of their actions in Contact Report #70 (updated report).

IDENTIFYING THE *WHAT ABOUT*

This section of the book is going to be a little tricky, you will need to keep an open mind and follow the theology and the practical reasoning of history, customs and interpretations. Within the vast amount of research that I have done on the "King List," I have found two sources that dare to mention UFOlogy relating to the Kings and the Sumerian Gods. Sometimes the question of extraterrestrial influence is never thought of, yet other times it seems like a far-fetched thought. If we step back and look at the total picture and try not to answer ALL the questions but just see the basic formation of events, the truth of it all is in "plain sight." With that said, let's work on the logic of the framework of the King List.

1. We see, as mentioned above, that the Antediluvian rulers "descended from heaven." Obviously they came to earth in flying ships of some sort for travel into outer space. They came for a period of time and then left before the Great Flood came (due to the Destroyer Comet of 8104 BC as previously presented), and then they returned after the flood when the destruction was over.

2. The time of the "Noah Flood" is in 8104 BC due to the fact that it was the most devastating flood and was worldwide.

3. The flood of 3453 BC did not pack the punch of devastation that the same comet did in 8,104 BC (came back every 575.5 years) because it was a "regional flood."

4. Artifacts that were carbon-dated to be between 2000 BC and 3000 BC (and only those found from that era) are erroneously thought of as the time of when the Kingship came to Earth. If that

were the case, the Noah Flood would not have happened since the Flood in 3453 BC was <u>regional</u> flood….not the <u>world</u> flood that occurred in 8104 BC.

5. If the Noah Flood in 3453 BC was a "world flood" as told in the Biblical Scripture, there would not be sufficient time for re-populating and building civilizations anew by the time other events happened in Sumerian and Mesopotamian history.

6. Only 8 people left the ark after the flood….and they had the task of re-populating the world and re-building civilizations.

7. The chronology of Sumerian activity needs to be moved back in time by 4651 years to the Noah flood of 8104 BC instead of ASSUMING that "this or that" took place since the Old Testament and Sumerian chronology charts do not have chronological dating that is correct as mentioned earlier in this work.

8. It must also be kept in mind that the Destroyer Comet in 8104 BC had such an effect on the earth (as previously mentioned) that the earth's axis was changed and its rotation increased which changed the length of a day from over 40 hours a day to 24 hours a day. <u>No mention of</u> those occurrences is recorded in the flood of 3453 BC. Therefore, the correct date for the Noah flood is 8104 BC.

At this point, we need to understand some history of the Sumerians as told in Contact Report #70 by Semjase (an advanced human female from Erra), that the Sumerians originally were peace-loving people. 133,000 years ago from the date of 1977, they settled in the areas of Pakistan, Persia, etc., but were attacked by a Jschwisch (Kang of Wisdom) by the name of Arus II in 11,000 BC. Jehovan, 3rd son of Arus XI, took over rulership of three groups. Descendents of Armus from 133,000 years ago who had emigrated from the Plejaren systems, a second group who were descendents of the Aryans who had mixed with humans who were pure Earthly, lethargic and a native population after the Sumerians were expelled. The third group was gypsies (travelers), eager to burn, murder and rob. They were called Hebrons based on the original language of their forefathers and were later called Hebraon and later Hebrons.[146]

---

146 Billy Meier, "Contact 70," *They Fly,* January 6, 1977, http://www.theyfly.com/.

After Jehovan ruled (third son of Arus XI), (then the BIBLICAL FLOOD), then camejehav, Arussem, Jehovah, Kamagol 1ˢᵗ, Kamagol 2ⁿᵈ, Ptaah and Salam, Salam, Plejos and then Jmmanuel. In the meantime, the Sumerians returned to their homeland to settle once again. At the end of Contact Report #70, it tells us that the Sumerians carried on mainly trade and agriculture because the Kingship had returned to the Universe and now the people's "knowledge and ability of a higher level and their origin disappeared into the darkness of forgetfulness."[147]

You will also note when reviewing the Chronology of the "Kingship" that came down to Earth after the Noah flood, due to the Destroyer Comet, that it had changed the length of the day from over 40 hours to a 24 hour day (See previous explanations of this matter in this work).

Before we tie-in the Hebrew history to Sumerian history, we need to understand the meaning of GOD. This title is explained by Semjase, one of the advanced humans from the planet of Erra in the 5ᵗʰ Contact Report, as "leaders very developed, and portrayed themselves to be Gods of man. They are called Kings of Wisdom, by the word IHWH/JHWH, which on Earth means GOD. Far superior to the ordinary people in spirit and knowledge, as well as in consciousness, they soon ruled it in an evil dictatorial form."[148]

So it is to be understood that the **Kingship were Gods in their own right,** not as common people. In the **definition of a GOD,** Semjase points out that the Kingship was far superior, which points to a highly intelligent position which at that point and time of history was not gained anywhere else neither in the world nor by any other means except through advanced extraterrestrial abilities. What is also pointed out through Contact #5 is that the Kingship was superior in the area of spiritual knowledge and growth. The Plejaren advocate this exact concept through the Billy Meier contact reports as well as the *Goblet of the Truth* which encompasses the Laws and Recommendations, which is to say the Teaching of the Truth, the Teaching of the Spirit and the Teaching of the Life.

The Kingship received their directives from the Gods, which once again is explained as the humans of superior abilities (i.e. scientists of many

---

[147]   Meier, "Contact 70."

[148]   Billy Meier, "Contact 5," *They Fly,* February 16, 1975, http://www.theyfly. com/.

disciplines) as explained in several instances in Contact Report #70.[149] This concept is also fostered by Daan Nijssen, author of Ancient Studies (2014), VU University Amsterdam.[150]

The Kingship/Gods would receive their direction from higher Gods in the same way that the Plejaren (the high technological humans from Erra) receive direction from the High Council which is located in the Andromeda Galaxy. In Contact #70, it is revealed to us that the council is comprised of semi-spiritual creatures, part human and part spiritual. The extraterrestrial nations of all races receive guidance, that is to say "high advice" instead of being ordered is available to any nation that joins the Federation.[151]

There are many lesser gods that were evident in households numbering in the hundreds in Sumeria. This will have a bearing on Abram's life as will be shown shortly.

Identifying the *Way It Ties In*

From here, we will look at how the Hebrews tie-in with the Sumerians. The use of a chronological time frame is useless as pointed out earlier in this work. But, the two dates that are a fact of Sumerian life and the Hebrew history are 8104 BC, the time of the Noah Flood that was caused by the Destroyer Comet, and the lesser flood caused by that same comet in 3453 BC.

A vast amount of detail and dates are lost due to the scribe (s) that left out the majority of genealogy from Adam to Jmmanuel which was mentioned previously. But, we will begin to appreciate more of the story of Abraham in Sumeria and the events that surround his life and families… and even clarify some myths.

Sumerian Gods

We are now once more reminded that the Sumerian Gods are simply humans of high intelligence in the areas of science and wisdom and are

---

[149] Billy Meier, "Contact 70," *They Fly,* January 6, 1977, http://www.theyfly.com/.

[150] Marie-Lan Nguyen, "Evolution of Sumerian Kingship," *Ancient World Magazine,* 2019, https://www.ancientworldmagazine.com/articles/evolution- sumerian-kingship/.

[151] Billy Meier, "Contact 70," *They Fly,* January 6, 1977, http://www.theyfly.com/.

commonly referred to as King of Wisdom, or IHWH, meaning Jschwjsch. In this word the "J" is pronounced as if it were an "I." The whole word would be phonetically pronounced as "Ishwish." A female King of Wisdom is called a Jschrjsch. Billy Meier explains this as well in the fact that the abbreviation "JHWH" is an Ancient Lyran term for King of Wisdom and that they are human beings like everybody else, but much higher in consciousness and spiritual development than average human beings. This, and other designations for God, appear such as Jahjeh, Jahawah, Jahve, Jahwe, Yahweh, Jehova, Jehovah, Jehowah, Adonai, Elohim, Ehjeh, LORD, Lord, HE, and Eternal One."[152]

Using this platform, the question comes forward "who really is Yahweh or Elohim?"

To discover and work with this question, we will begin in Sumeria and we will begin with Abram, or more commonly known as Abraham, and the place of his birth, Ur of the Chaldeans. The city was along the Euphrates River on the edge of the Alajarah Desert. Today, it is known as Tall al Mugayyar, Iraq.

Dating of Abram's birth is useless since the timeline of what has been published is off by approximately 575.5 years as previously pointed out due to the fact that scientists, researchers and the like did not study the Destroyer Comet which caused the Noah Flood and when it came, which was in 8104 BC, not the erroneous date of 3453 BC when the Destroyer Comet came and did much less damage as a "regional" flood instead of a world flood.

After Noah died in Gen. 9, his descendents moved and ended up in the Plain of Shinar between Babylon and Ur as listed in Genesis 10 and 11 (KJV). The family must have set up their home very close to Ur or had eventually moved to Ur since Genesis 11:28 tell us that Abram's brother Haran died "in the land of his nativity, in Ur of the Chaldees. In Genesis 11:31 (KJV) it also tells us that Abram's father and family left from "Ur" and moved to the city of Haran where Abram's father died.

Since Abram was in Sumeria, specifically Ur, the influence of a God was prevalent, (which previously was pointed out to be the Kingship and defined by the Plejaren as a highly technological human from elsewhere in

---

[152]   Billy Meier, "JHWH," *Ohio Exopolitics Radio Show,* accessed January 21, 2019, http://www.exopoliticsohio.us/Billy Meier.html.

the universe), the question here is what God is being addressed and what about a belief in a god by his forefathers?

It was pointed out earlier in this work by Billy Meier's main teacher, Semjase, that a God is only a "governor and moreover a human being." This throws a whole new light on the fact that God, or Lord God of mankind, is just a human of high intellect and knowledge of science and technology.

We find in Joshua 24:2 (KJV) that Joshua calls Israel (their name at that time had all ready been established as Israel) together and reminds them of how their forefathers before Abraham, including Abraham's father Terah and Abraham's grandfather Nahor served other "gods." We see that the gods of Mesopotamia were a very real part of Abraham's own relatives when his nephew Laban (his brother Nahor's son) had in his possession the images (gods) that Rachel had formerly stolen from her father, Genesis 31:19 (KJV). The trouble spills over into verse 34 and ends in Genesis 35:2 (KJV) when Jacob said to his "household and to all that were with him, put away these strange gods that are among you,…"

These gods were the lesser gods made of clay or wood compared to the Kingship that consisted of greater gods. But really, isn't this exactly like society today? Everybody has their "god" or "gods" of preference and priority such as money, material goods, fame and etc.? This will be looked at in more depth later.

It comes down to the fact that God, the human of high intellect in technology and science, was not in agreement with humans worshiping lesser gods as in graven images referred to in Genesis 35:2 (KJV). The Biblical Scripture even states that God is a jealous God, Exodus 20:3-5 (KJV), as recorded in the Ten Commandments, and states that no other gods should come before Him, no graven images of other gods be made and no serving other gods.

This short analysis proves that the worshiping of a god or gods is, or can be, a strong issue. But this was not always the case. We see in Genesis 4:26 (KJV) that mankind did not begin to call upon the Lord until Seth had a son by the name of Enos. The term "Lord" was used in this sense as the proper name of the Hebrew God Yehovah/ Jehovah.

Before we examine the meaning and significance of the term Yehovah/ Jehovah, we need to finish up the analysis of just who did or did not believe in a god, of different levels such as the lesser gods that were household gods made of clay or wood, gods who were of the Kingship that came to Earth, and finally what would be defined as a higher God. We will see this shortly in a comparison with the Plejaren and their levels of authority.

For now, we need to follow the genealogy going back in time from Abraham to Adam. The specifics of Adam and Eve's coming on the scene of life are different than what the Bible tells us and will be dealt with shortly. For now, and for purposes of seeing matters from a Biblical stance so that those that believe in the Bible can see there is a greater lineage and timeline than what is presented in the Bible as well as the influence of advanced humans from elsewhere in the universe have a greater and a more corrected correlation to who and what we are today.

The following are the generations from Adam to Abraham which is what has been stated by the highly advanced humans from Erra that have imparted this information in the Talmud of Jmmanuel. As stated previously, many of the names are not in the Bible which further testifies to the fact that the greater list of generations must be recorded and taken into account to fulfill the dating of patriarchs, the factual existence and devastating effect of the Destroyer Comet, as previously covered in relationship to the account of the worldwide flood.

- Adam, Seth, and Enos—believers in the Biblical God.
- Akjbeel, Aruseak, Kenan, Mahalaleel, Urakjbarameel, Jared—Missing in the Biblical genealogy and of unknown belief.
- Henoch—believer in the Biblical God, and taken "up" by
- the Biblical God so he would not experience earthly death, Genesis 5:22 and Hebrews 11:5 (KJV).
- Methusalah—believer in the Biblical God (his Hebrew
- name means "worshiper of the deity")
- Hamech (Lamech)—believer in the Biblical God. He Testified of God's curse of the ground, and mankind's relief of it through the "toil of our hands." Genesis 5:29 (KJV)
- Tamjel, Danel, Asael, Samsafeel, Jomjael, Turel—Missing in the Biblical genealogy and of unknown belief.
- Noah—believer in the Biblical God.
- Sem—believer in the Biblical God.

- Arpachsad, Batrael, Ramuel, Askeel, Amers, Salah— Missing in the Biblical genealogy and of unknown belief.
- Eber—Presumably a believer in the Biblical God. In Luke
- 3:23-38 (KJV) he is listed as the great, great grandson of Sem (Shem). Eber's father Salah is listed but his grandfather and his great grandfather **is missing** from Luke 3:35- 38 (KJV).
- Peleg—unknown belief.
- *Regu unknown belief.
- Serug—believer in idols.[153]
- *Araseal—unknown belief.
- Nahor—as a child he believed in polytheism; later as a
- child he converted to the Biblical God.[154]
- *Thara—believer in idols.
- *Abram—believer in the Biblical God.

From the explanations above it is plain to see that not everyone in this section of the genealogical list followed the Biblical God. Moving on from here and accepting this fact, what was it that made Abraham choose a God of the other monotheistic religion? After all, he could have followed the Kingship that existed or any of the graven images at that time.

In Genesis 12:1-3, we see that Abraham receives a call from the "Lord" which is not defined as to how this is accomplished. Not by mail, telegram or phone of any type…but by mental telepathy! To understand the possibility of that type of communication, we have to keep an open mind, yes LOOK OUTSIED THE BOX!!!!!!

In the early years of Billy Meier's life, age 5, is when he initially heard a voice in his head. It was the first contact of an advanced technological human from the Pleiades, the first of many years ahead that were to be not only through mental telepathy….but also in person.[155]

This is not so different than Abraham; we just have to get our scope of history tuned into the fact that we are not the first humans in the past several thousand years to be faced with a sudden reality that history

---

[153]   R. H. Charles, *The Apocrypha and Pseudepigrapha of the Old Testament,* ed. Joshua Williams (Clarendon Press, 1913), http://www.pseudepigrapha.com/ jubilees/1 l.htm.

[154]   Charles, *The Apocrypha and Pseudepigrapha of the Old Testament.*

[155]   Billy Meier, "Age 5: The First Meeting and Awareness," *Semjase,* April 5, 2006, http:// www. semj ase.net.

REALLY IS NOT what is put into high school or college text books as myths!!!

Out of the several levels of deities, **the lowest levels of deity are the idols** fashioned of stone, clay, or wood. **The next level up is an IHWH/JHWH,** meaning King of Wisdom and though they are humans, they can be thought of as "Gods" because of their high abilities in the areas of science and technology. This terminology of God would be that of Immanuel (aka Jesus) an IHWH/JHWH. The **highest level of a "God"** is the human that has reached a spiritual level likened to those on the High Council as described in Contact #70. It is revealed to us that the council is comprised of semi-spiritual creatures, part human and part spiritual.[156] This terminology of God would be applied to "God the Father."

The big question is WHO IS JEHOVAH GOD? In this question are two things that need pointing out. The term "God" is in reference to a position, while the term "Jehovah" is a personage.

To set the background, we need to understand from The Chronology of Earth History chart, seen previously in this work, states that the city of Atlantis is founded about 31,000 BC and the great city of Mu is founded about 30,500 BC. In 9,498 BC Atlantis and Mu destroyed each other and the air is not suitable to breathe and the remaining humans scatter for safety and shelter.

Fifty years later an IHWH/JHWH by the name of Jehovan, 3rd son of an IHWH/JHWH called Arns XI, takes charge in **9448 BC** of the three remaining tribes left on earth. The first group consisted of descendants of an IHWH/JHWH named Armus. The second group consisted of descendants from another IHWH/JHWH by the name of Arus who were from the areas of India, Pakistan, Persia and surrounding areas. The third group was a rag-tag bunch of rabble-rousers that focused on greed through murder, burning and robbing known as the Hebraons by the ancient language and then Hebrons to the final designation of Hebrews. After Jehovan's rulership was taken by Jehav in **5,000 BC,** he was murdered by his first son Arussem. Arussem took leadership but was expelled through the efforts of his sons Ptaah and Salam. He later returned to Earth and resided with his followers 3,000 to 4,000 meters under the Pyramids in Egypt until **3,010 BC.** In the meantime one of the followers of Arussem,

---

[156] Billy Meier, "Contact 70," *They Fly,* January 6, 1977, http://www.theyfly.com/.

by the name of Henn (who was called Jehovah and nicknamed "The Unjust Cruel one") left Arussem's group and took over leadership of the tribes. He was later displaced by a nephew of his by the name of Kamagol 1st and forced all religions to obey him, created cults and demanded human blood. His son Kamagol 2nd, a very vicious person, overthrew his father and put him in a dungeon where he eventually died. The remaining two sons of Jehav, Ptaah and Salam, took rulership by common agreement. Ptaah passes away at age 93 and the command is given to Plejos, the son of Ptaah, in **63 BC** who then places himself and his people after a period of time under the guidance of spiritual leaders of his home form of government namely the "High Council. Plejos returned to his homeworlds in **17 BC.**"[157]

To sum it up, all these personages are IHWH/JHWH which is to say a King of Wisdom, or simply "God," and eventually pass away while another IHWH/JHWH (God) takes over. Henn, who was labeled the "Unjust Cruel one" and called himself "Jehovah," passed away 2,150 years prior to the 39th contact which was on December 3, 1975. His passing would have been in **175 BC.**[158]

The conclusion to this is that the God of the Bible, IHWH/JHWH, is none other than a human of high technological and scientific knowledge that even today is worshiped by Hebrews and Christians of all avenues of Christianity (even though he is dead) resulting in the **world's greatest DELUSION.**

---

[157]   Meier, "Contact 70."
[158]   Meier, "Contact 70."

CHAPTER 4

System of Introduction and Influence

We are introduced to religious beliefs in various ways. Many times it is through the influence of other people by means of personal contact such as by someone sitting next to you in a work environment dining area and begins a conversation relating to daily life and eternity. It could be through a tract, meaning a small piece of paper that has a single, bi-fold or tri-fold configuration that poses a question, uses Biblical scripture to prove the point in question, and then introduces the solution to topics in life including after-life. The purpose of this approach is to get you to think, develop some ideas and thoughts, then to form a dialogue through talking, mail, email, invitation to a religious gathering, teaching session or special presentation.

What really matters is where is a person being led into?

<u>The Professional Approach</u>—People are fed remarks that confuse them or present a matter of doubt in their mind. Many times people who appear "in style" or have good verbal expertise can have an influence of "professionalism" and "knowing what they are saying." This approach brings a sense of excitement to the listener as if there is no other belief to consider except what has been presented.

<u>I've got the Answer Approach</u>—This approach focuses on counseling people that are going through troubles and trials but not finding anything that satisfies their condition. Many times this approach comes in the form of "this is the answer to all your troubles." The real condition here is that the inquiring person is getting their neck stroked and their ear scratched with sympathetic responses in order to gain the trust of the inquiring person.

Everybody else is wrong approach—You ever hear them say "we are the true believers" or our group has the answer, you will never go wrong" with the beliefs we have. The question to ask here is "who made your group, church, denomination or whatever organization that is being referred to as being the only one or ones the answer to all questions.

Scare tactic approach—This approach focuses on questions that appeal to living somewhere beyond death and uses questions such as "don't you want to live forever?" Or, "wouldn't you want to spend eternity with your loved ones?" Or, "you know that there is a place of burning and eternal torture if you don't believe in what I am saying!"

Talent approach—In this approach, the beliefs of the religious organization are not the main focus, but the seeking of them as an asset to the organization. Remarks such as "you are really great in you organizational skill, teaching skills, etc., we sure could use someone like you!" Immediately the listener is excited because someone sees something in them such as a talent or skill and it pumps the listener up to the point of saying "yes" when they haven't even considered what the organization is about.

The asset approach—Many times people are introduced to a religious organization because of the materialistic assets and financial supply that a person has. Comments may come out similar to "we sure could use your financial backing to do this or that. The listener needs to back off and ask themselves "what does this organization want of me?"

Last but not least is the "This book, the Bible, has all the answers, Jesus will never fail you" approach.—Within this approach are statements such as "prayer changes things," and "Jesus will guide you all the way," or "Jesus never fails."

Regardless of the above approaches, there was a time when you accepted some wild and unbelievable stories contained within the Bible or religious book of said religion. Week after week you would hear explanations of the Bible or religious book you were taught as being faithful and true in its content until over the years you finally accepted it as the truth…you never challenged it to see if it was indeed true!

INTERPRETATION

Let's look at an example, a true one, about the Bible. It involves the passage in Isaiah 7:10-17 (KJV). Many would say that the term *Immanuel* in verse 14 is in reference to Jesus Christ, yet Jesus is not mentioned at all, nor is Immanuel mentioned in the account of the virgin birth, nor is the proclamation of him coming to "save his people from their sins," Matthew 1:21 (KJV).

In fact, the original Dead Sea Scrolls, which are about 1,000 years older than the Hebrew Bible,[159] testify of differences between the Masoretic version of Isaiah and the version found in Qumran.

We see in the approximately 1,000 year older manuscript from the "Dead Sea Scrolls" for instance that in Isaiah 7:14 the wording is "Behold, a virgin shall conceive," when it should rightfully read "a young woman, girl or unmarried maiden," *almah* in Hebrew. The twist here is that the assumption is made that the young woman is also a virgin.

Another concern is in Isaiah 7:15-16 (KJV) where the coming child, called Jesus in Matthew 1:21 (KJV), is presented as not knowing good or evil as a child. There is a real discrepancy here in theology! If Immanuel/Jesus is not of sufficient discretion to know "good from evil" as a child and it is something he has to learn to differentiate, then the reality is that Immanuel is a human. Not only does Isaiah 7:15 (KJV) affirm that he is indeed a human, and would become a JHWH (King of Wisdom) but he would share co-rulership with the personage of a senior God, in Isaiah 9:6 and would be likened to as a "Father" from a human perspective.

We also find in Matthew 1:23 (KJV) that the child would be called "Immanuel," which contradicts verse 21 which states that the child's name is "Jesus"…a name that was never identified in the Old Testament. And, the name Immanuel/Jmmanuel should actually be interpreted "he of godly knowledge," referring to the "knowledge of an Jshwjsh" (JHWH) denoting "a human with extremely high learning, of an initiated and wise counselor."[160]

---

[159] "English Translations of the Book of Isaiah," *The Digital Dead Sea Scrolls,* trans. Prof Peter W. Flint and Prof Eugene Ulrich of Isaiah of the Dead Scrolls, accessed February 2, 2019, http://dss.collections.imj.org.il/chapters_pg.

[160] Hans Lanzendorfer, "Clarification of a Defamatory Claim," *They Fly,* accessed February 4, 2019, http://www.theyfly.com/articles/Clarification_of_a_ Defamatory_Claim.html.

To understand this and many other revelations of what the Truth is, Billy Meir reveals the dialogue that he had with Immanuel/ Jmmanuel when going back in time with an advanced human from the DAL Universe. Oh by the way, this is not comic book stuff because if you read the Bible, especially the Book of Revelation, there are revelations in it that are more far-out than when I am imparting in this book.

Getting back to Billy's conversation, Immanuel/Jmmanuel testifies that the Pharisees and Scribes have falsified the writings of the Bible…and, God is a creature of Creation as all of us are. God is a King of Wisdom (just as I pointed out previously in the Sumerian's believing in Gods) and that a King of Wisdom is just a ruler over human races in the same application as a king or emperor rules over human races on Earth.[161]

Immanuel continues his conversation with Billy by pointing out that the texts are being falsely modified, false claims are being put into his mouth as if he (Immanuel/Jmmanuel) had consorted with someone called "his father in heaven," even the lie that God is the creator. Humans have been "beaten" into servitude and enslaved in dogmas through exploited evil ways. The Truth is that PEOPLE MUST BE FREE OF MISLEADING INFORMATION (which Christianity and other off-shoots of it have become a cult) AND THE DOGMAS/FALSE TEACHINGS! Immanuel/ Jmmanuel sums it up by stating "A religious teaching itself can only be valuable and instructive if it is free of dogmas and human false teachings as well as other nonsense,…"[162]

In fact, the best way to realize the Truth is to read it in what is called the Talmud of Jmmanuel. This writing is the correct communique of what was known as the Gospel of Matthew. The history of how it came into the hands of Billy Meier is recorded in it as well a commentary of the script in understanding its teaching. The script and historical explanations can be purchased in hard cover through http:/1 www.theyfly.com/.

---

[161] Billy Meier, "Askets Explanations Part 8," *They Fly,* October 2009, http://www. theyfly.com/.

[162] Meier, "AsLet's Explanations Part 8."

God

This leads to another question. We have already stated that there is no "so-called" God that has created everything. A God is a human being with exceptional knowledge and advancement that claims ruler-ship over human-kind. Well then, who or what created what is in existence today?

This question was brought by Billy Meier to Semjase, a woman advanced in science and technology from the planet Erra. The explanation that she gives sounds much like the Christian God...but is not God. The reason why mankind will have trouble with how Semjase explains Creation is because mankind is "relational." Mankind has a need to relate to someone or something in order to express feelings such as gratitude, help and for counseling which in essence is simple. The proper scope of a relational approach is for the human to have a relationship with their Spirit to help it grow. That subject is dealt with shortly.

Semjase points out that everything in the universe is made of matter and has energy. There is the coarse-substantial, like holding a rock, and there is the fine-fluidal which is energy. In a nut shell, Creation, which is pure Spirit, embodies primal energy. It takes an idea and "compresses and concentrates the idea to fine-fluidal energy, but then is condensed to a higher concentration into coarse-substantial and becoming matter. Beyond this explanation Semjase claims she and her people do not know further explanations."[163] Further reading of "Understanding the Term *Creation*" can be found in Contact Report 18.[164]

Creation

Creation has always been a deep subject and creates wonderment in the minds of human beings. In Christianity humankind are told in summary that Creation is all that exists and is created by intelligent design, meaning God.

Billy Meier (7th and last Prophet), explains that all of what exists is created by intelligent design, an "immense, neutral energetical and

---

[163] Meier, "Askets Explanations Part 8."
[164] Billy Meier, "Understanding Creation, Contact 18," *They Fly*, May 15, 1975, http://www. theyfly. com/.

evolutive BEING as a pure natural state of energy, a natural evolutive spirit-energetical activity-energy, and therefore not a *wesen* (German: being or creature) in the sense of a human being, other creature or other personified *wesen* (German: being or creature), therefore also not a divinity in superhuman form."[165] Further descriptions of Creation can be found in the explanations by Billy Meier titled "What is the Creation?"[166]

Though the explanations of the character of Creation and how we can relate to it are majestic, the question is asked "how does Creation really take place?" Billy Meier addresses the issue of the "process of Creation" to Semjase, a lady of great scientific understanding who is over 300 years old. She addresses the fact that "Matter is a tangible idea and that it is a solid form of energy that is tangible. Each energy can be changed in solid matter. She then explains energy can be changed through highly focused and concentrated means. The change involves solid matter, neutron, proton and electron. Matter is the embodiment of an idea, and the force of the spirit (which in turn embodies energy) compresses and concentrates the idea to fine-fluidal energy and in turn condensed through a still higher concentration into coarse-substantial, to matter.[167] The explanation given in Contact Report#8 is absolutely awesome and will take the reader some pondering and re-reading to fully appreciate the true approach to Creation by Intelligent Design.

There is another contact report that deals with the creation of mankind specifically of which space for discussion here does not lend itself. It can be accessed online at FIGU Special Bulletin #32 Translation and explains that mankind did not descend from ape-beings, but from one single primal lineage.

Religious Teachings

Of note once again is that mankind must be free from the dogmas of religion. This entails the cultish teachings of "you must do this" or

---

[165] Billy Meier, "What is Creation," *They Fly*, accessed February 15, 2019, http:// www. theyfly.com/spiritual/What_Is_the_Creation.html.

[166] Billy Meier, "What is the Creation," *Stime der Wassermannzeit (Voice of the Aquarian)*, no. 89 (December 1993), https://ca.figu.org/what-is-the-creation-. html.

[167] Billy Meier, "Contacts," *They Fly*, March 18, 1975, http://www.theyfly.com/.

you "must do that" to please a God and receive forgiveness for sins. In association to this topic are non-biblical do's and don'ts that mankind must do to be blessed by the Biblical God. Examples are baptism, confession to a priest, certain hand gestures forming the sign of the cross, icons of saints on car dashboards and necklaces, the lighting of candles, fraternities that represent the church or allegiance to God, participation in activities that imitate the suffering of Jesus, and the practice of drinking of the cup (referred to as Communion or Eucharist) supposedly representing the blood of Jesus. By the way, that cup is exactly what the various Gods (because they were led by different ones from time to time) of the Hebrews were required in the way of blood sacrifice from the Old Testament for atonement which also translated to the supposed death of Jesus on the cross as a mode of remembrance.[168]

This type of environment among denominations and religions had resulted in a great consternation as to people following these instructions like sheep going to slaughter. They caused dissention with those who do not have convictions of those practices and it puts enmity between people because of one stating (i.e. religious leaders) that another MUST do these things in order to follow church teachings and receive grace and blessings from God.

Forgiveness

The crux of this topic entails forgiveness and one's ability to face accountability. You don't need to ask forgiveness from a God, that's a cop-out! You need to take the bull by the horns and admit it was your fault and learn to see your accountability in the relationships you have with mankind. Go to the other person (s) and seek their forgiveness. Learn the value of mended relationships as well as the mending of yourself. No God can force two people to come together and deal with forgiveness, you and the other person need to do it because it is a vital part of building internal integrity as well as outward respectability.

Excuses such as "I'll just let it blow over," or "it's really not my fault" when you are trying to dodge the bullet of accountability. I have seen this

---

168   Billy Meier, "Contact 70," *They Fly,* January 6, 1977, http://www.theyfly.com/.

time and time again with friends, neighbors, relatives, co-workers and mostly those that claim they are brothers and sisters in their religious beliefs.

Why is this so? I have found that Christians tend to elevate themselves more-so than the general public because they are "Christians" as if to say that they are better than a non-Christian. They look down on the "heathen" non-believers as if to say "I'm going to Heaven and you aren't!" It's time to stop the God-factor, church-factor, religious attitude factor, heaven and hell factor, and religious dogma factors and create peace, instead of religious animosity through the teachings of the Goblet of the Truth.

Many times a pro-active stand to go to the other person, regardless of the so-called "fault," results in putting off the desire to square things away as if God knows you would like to do so and it appeases you that at least God knows your intent. Sorry, that doesn't settle anything. Remove the God-factor and contact the other party and meet with them in a humble attitude so that relationships can be mended. If it fails because the other person refuses to meet or does not want to reconcile, at least you have made the attempt. Make sure you keep the door of opportunity open for future meetings with them. It is not God that's going to move their heart…it's you by making known to them that you value the relationship.

Relying on a God to bring people together is a smoke-screen for personal responsibility. When you bring a God into the equation the attitude becomes "well, I'll wait until God moves their heart. Or, "I've done my part; I'll just set back and let God do his part." Wait a minute! God was never a part of the dissention that caused you and the other person to have a disagreement, why would you depend on God to solve the matter? Pull up your big-boy pants and make the effort!

Many times I have seen it happen between brothers and sisters, children and parents and even between spouses…when in fact it is one of the first places humble forgiveness should take place. We are not all the same and that's why we need to show and practice positive forgiveness toward all mankind.

One of the greatest acts of unrighteousness in Christianity is the unforgiving attitude and actions of people in the Christian churches and in family units due to a divorce, crime, abandonment, misunderstanding and false accusations. These situations lead to three horrible actions.

1. Complete separation from the offending person (s), called "avoidance."

    I have seen this time and time again, especially those that are conservative Biblical Christians who "think" that they are "in the right" and refuse to come to the table with the other person (s) to settle a matter in humility. Why? Because they think that their position as a Bible believing Christian is their sword and shield when in reality they use their sword to kill their fellow man and their shield to block the humility they should be living. They think they are "above" the other person in their faith just because they claim "God is my refuge and strength," and claim they follow Biblical teachings. And by the way, this goes beyond Christianity to other religious groups whether Muslim, Hindu, Buddhist, etc.

    The unique teaching of the *Goblet of the Truth,* finally put into written text by Billy Meier (the last of the seven prophets) after thousands and thousands of years, teaches us that no one is above another. We are responsible for ourselves and in our relationships toward others. The Goblet of the Truth focuses on our person-to-person relationships, not a God-to-person! A person may say that they are following the teachings of a God, but then uses that relationship through twisting and ignoring the precepts of that God. A God becomes a crutch, and even an entity to avoid at-will. When we remove the God from whatever belief system exists, we have no deity as a crutch and we can focus entirely on person to person relationships as taught in the Goblet of the Truth.

2. Back-stabbing of each party.

    Verbal fighting is as damaging as physical fighting and it can damage relationships for years, and even until death. A belief system such as Christianity is a farce and I hear it almost daily in language such as "if they were Christians' they wouldn't act like that," or "if that's what Christianity is all about, I don't want any part of it."

3. Inward lying.

When I use to be a youth and family counselor several years ago, I loved to work with kids that had Aspergers, an Autistic spectrum disorder, because you always knew how they felt since they love to be verbal about their thoughts. Sometimes I think how wonderful it would be to know people's thoughts instead of them pretending or hiding their agenda towards relationships so that they can be out on the table and dealt with. It's time to get the God-issue off the table and face the "here and now" about the inward prejudices, grudges, schemes, etc. and deal with what is within. One of the worst applications is how Christians claim that they believe every verse in the Bible, yet fail to apply it and then live an inward lie.

Shame on our society for not teaching and practicing these attributes form the foundation of who we should be as humans. When you read the history of civilizations that have been established in the thousands of years in the past as written in Contact Report #70 located on http://www. theyfly.com/, you see greed for power, lust, prejudice, hate, and selfishness among leaders and eventually the followers.

So the question from the depths of the universe is "how do we rectify this disease of religious delusion?"

I have already stated that the God-issue needs to be removed from the table.

Start serving one another without the distraction of a God.

Seek to understand from the other persons' point of view.

Treat others as valuable in the sight of Creation.

Never look at yourself as better than anyone else in spite of your education, talents and skills or lineage. Our society is too focused on idols, heroes, awards, trophies, titles, etc. If we focus on people to the point that they become icons and then that icon commits a crime, where does the belief in that so-called star fall? I'm not saying that you can't use a talented person's efforts as a blueprint for your own guide, but what I'm saying is don't hold people of great talent so high that they become a god unto you. The highest reward we can bring is peace, and it should reign within us…. that should be enough! Once again, I refer you to the *Goblet of the Truth* as your guide to the Creational Laws and Recommendations.

ETERNAL LIFE

The last subject to be covered in the dogmas of belief, and in particular with those that have a belief in a God or Savior, is the matter of eternal life. There are two particular teachings about this subject that attract people to religion

1. The reward of being with loved ones in Heaven.
2. To have life eternal.

The first false teaching of having loved ones in Heaven is contrary to the laws of life and death which is referred to many times in the *Goblet of The Truth* and in the teachings of Billy Meier (the 7th and last prophet) as the "coming and passing." Death is a finality of Creation. In "clinical" death, the brain still has electrical activity, but in "brain" death" the person is fully dead.[169] In addition, there is no heaven or hell, as is stated to Billy Meier, by Semjase in Contact Report #6.[170] This is also spoken of many times in the *Goblet of the Truth* whereby each person creates a Heaven or Hell within themselves through the way they handle life, themselves and others.

In other words, Heaven and Hell are not places but rather a condition in you.[171] Further comments about Heaven or Hell can be accessed through the website of where on the left side of the main page you can scroll down to see the entire *Goblet of the Truth* for free and you can also use the "Index to the *Goblet of the Truth* to look up specific topics such as Heaven or Hell.

To be clear, yet in a nutshell, humans do not have a soul, just a Spirit which is located in the region of the Superior Colliculus near the top of the brain stem. The Spirit of the human is immortal and it escapes into its realm of the other-world in order to be reborn in due time when a new human body is born with a new consciousness, subconscious and new personality. A great explanation of the human Spirit (or Spirit-form as it is referred to), its abode after death, its re-birth into a new human and

---

[169]   Jacob Smits, "Death, Afterlife, and Rebirth," *They Fly*, accessed February 6, 2019, http://www.futureoffmankind.co.uk/Billy_Meier/Death_Afterlife_and Rebirth.

[170]   Billy Meier, "Contact 6," *They Fly*, February 23, 1975, http://www.theyfly.com.

[171]   Billy Meier, *Goblet of the Truth* (Canada: FIGU-Landsgruppe Canada, 2015).

its process of maturity in ages to come from person to person is expertly detailed in a 25 page dissertation by Billy Meier. It is simply fantastic![172]

When you remove the "God factor" of restrictions and requirements, it allows the human to focus on the development of his/her Spirit so that the Spirit can incarnate in future humans and grow in wisdom through the several levels of development. The realization here is that each person has a personal relationship with their Spirit, and how each person conducts their life in learning through good judgment, rational living, logical choices, self-control, using the right perspective of love, the fostering of peace and harmony toward mankind and the respect and preservation of and for Creation.

Sin

This topic may be one of the more problematic topics in each of our lives since there are twists to it in Christianity that subject a person to fear and anxiety as well as questionable living.

The matter of "original sin" comes to us in the historical account of highly developed humans from the Sirius regions that were genetically-manipulated who came to earth after leaving Mars due to uninhabitable cosmic influences. Thousands of people were genetically-manipulated by the over-lords and resulted in people who ended up having great fighting powers, yet yielded an adverse effect on them such as becoming very old and dying prematurely. Their whole demeanor changed due to the manipulation of genes whereby they had a penchant to fight. They became vicious, barbaric, blood thirsty, greedy, and addicted to mayhem, emotionalism and inhumanities. This became what was called the "original sin."[173]

Information regarding "original sin" was erroneously proclaimed by Christian religions as the fable of Adam and Eve and the serpent in the Garden of Eden. The whole situation is founded on the manipulation of a

---

[172]   Billy Meier, "Life, Death, and Rebirth," trans. Kate Bergheim, December 9, 2012, http://www.meiersaken.info/Reinkarnation.html.

[173]   Billy Meier, "Contact 251," *They Fly,* February 3, 1995, http://www.theyfly. com.

single DNA gene that can be remedied if geneticists today were to finally discover it.[174]

In the Goblet of the Truth our wrong actions toward self and others are referred to as "errors" as a non-religious term. This is an important issue to cover since it dominates the lives of mankind and has created untold chaos throughout the world. The below explanations,[175] come from the Goblet of the Truth, the page is number is listed first, then the chapter and verse.

Errors— (throwbacks)—they reveal to us the incorrect ways of our life so we can change them to the good. The reason they are called throwbacks is because the errors that we commit throw us back from moving forward in truth and our personal growth. Page 583, Chapter 28:560-561, page 461, Chapter 25:241-243, Page 283, Chapter 9:19.

Errors—are able to prevent another from committing misdeeds. In other words, the errors a person commits can serve as an example to themselves and others of what went wrong and how it can be avoided in the future. Page 187, Chapter 5:101; page 169, Chapter 5:22; page 181, Chapter 5:75.

Errors—against others can be reconciled through apologies and amends. Page 503, Chapter 28:76.

Errors—changing your life to obtain peace, harmony& freedom within. Page313, Chapter 10:48-54. Page417, Chapter 23:165.

Errors—guidelines for punishment. Page 195, Chapter 5:137.

Errors—fight against with positive thought-forms with energy/power in your feelings, will& volition. Page 461, Chapter 25:244-245.

Errors—bad deeds are not punished by a god or tin gods. Page 171, Chapter 5:33.

Errors— (what religion calls "sin") cleansed through the application of the Truth. Page 325; Chapter 11:40. Learn from it and rise above the matter. Page 583, Chapter 28:560.

Errors— (wrong doing) turn away from and trust in the Laws and Recommendations. Page 305, Chapter 9:129.

So what do we learn and apply from this topic of 'Errors?" We need to remove the God-factor and be responsible for ourselves. When the God-factor is applied it is easy to state a confessional prayer and quickly

---

[174]   Meier, "Contact 251."

[175]   Billy Meier, *Goblet of the Truth* (Canada: FIGU-Landsgruppe Canada, 2015).

dismiss it from our thoughts. It portrays a quick "get it over" approach when it should be a matter of self-contemplation, self-examination and self-rectification as to the wrong-doing and action to not commit the "error" again. God is not going to sit down at the table with a cup of coffee or can of pop and counsel you on the matter. You have to face the guilt, hurt, and separation between you and the other person (s) and work it through with honest and respectful talk.

The process begins with forgiving yourself as you speak to your personal Spirit, not going to a God or Savior. It is your responsibility to forgive yourself of your own "Error" and forgive the other people because it involves only those people, not a God or Savior. You have a brain, a heart, and the ability to reason out matters and use logic to follow through with the decision and goal of reconciliation.

If other people do not want to work it out, then at least you have made the effort. Express sensitivity with other people so that the door of communication hopefully will stay open.

CHAPTER 5

Expectations of Delusion

In the study of a God that rules the world and imparts "good" and "bad" at his bidding, the Christian fails to see the total picture of the history of the Universe and the involvement of mankind in it. What the Christian experiences is actually the "here and now" of what they have been taught that narrows mankind's scope of reality. From here, we break into some Apologetics and digress about the existence and non-existence of a God that is claimed to be omnipresent (all present), omniscient (all knowing) and omnipotent (all powerful).

Delusion: Myths

In this writing, it has been shown and proven through documentation the existence <u>of advanced humans as being Gods</u> that have come down to earth and led mankind, such as in the case of the Sumerians as recorded in the King List previously mentioned. The length of reign that each of them had clearly shows they had the capacity to live not only for hundreds of years but thousands of years. Why would science and religionists look at this data and call it a myth? The answer lies in the restricted thinking of what is before them and claiming it doesn't sound reasonable! Yet the Christian accepts the unreasonable events in the Bible because they are defending "their Bible" that they believe in as well as a God that doesn't exist. Therefore, as more history is studied about myths, especially in the realms of UFOlogy, the more they are showing to be true.

95

For those that do not accept the examination of facts and the explanations that are revealed, it explicitly shows not only a narrow mindedness but a complete refusal to look at the broader issues of history in the past that has revealed ancient revelations of mankind from other parts of our universe.

Those outside of Christianity would look at it and call the Bible a myth because of various events and people that seem to them as being false. The revelations of the Plejaren and their message to mankind through Billy Meier have all ready been spread throughout the world and will continue to reach mankind by using education, rationality and logic in discerning the Truth revealed in the *Goblet of the Truth.*

Delusion: Accept Only Biblical Say-So

So here is the Delusion of Religion! A person is expected to accept so-called miracles and divine incidents from the Bible, yet not accept the reality of advanced humans from another planet visiting earth or of the fact that advanced humans really DID inhabit Mars at one time.[176] Why is this so? The answer that religionists give is that the Bible did not say it was so! That my friend is the Delusion of Religion!

If this is a person's answer, then obviously they will look at only what they personally believe in or what they have been taught and will judge everything else the same way…except when it comes to their own convictions about a religious belief that they hold onto. This approach is nothing more than narrow-mindedness. Why, because if a person says that they believe everything from cover to cover in the Bible, then it makes a liar of them due to the fact that anything outside the Bible they will claim as false. Why, because dramatic events within the Bible and outside the Bible are no different….they happened without any deity controlling them.

Delusion: Deity Determines Your Life

Let's review this a little closer in the realm of another law…the law of "natural progression." This can be seen in the events of life whether

---

[176]   Billy Meier, "Contact 251," *They Fly,* February 3, 1995, http://www.theyfly.com.

individually or in a global setting, in peace time or in war. I remember a gentleman that I met in the late 1960's that was part of a unit on a hill in Vietnam consisting of approximately 100 men. When the fighting was over, there were only five men that survived. The soldier's big question was "why was I allowed to survive?" Many religionists replied "because God has a plan for you." The fallacy in their statement is that a God does not determine the plan for your life…you create the results by accessing your desire to be what you want to be and the steps that you have to initiate and follow through to go to college, choose a mate, buy a car, a place to rent or buy, etc, etc.

People from his church stated that God has a plan for you, be patient and he will answer your prayers. This dear soldier, like so many other people in Christianity, were left in a delusion because they never got off their painted pony of prayer and realized that they needed to develop themselves in self-confidence, self-assurance, developing priorities and setting up a life-plan with a step by step plan on reaching a goal (s).

The delusion of a God supplying all of your needs is false and misleading. Every person needs to understand that if they are going to accomplish what they wish to succeed in takes self-effort. O.k., let's apply some of this Christian discipline here when Paul writes about some lazy Christians in II Thessalonians 3:7-1 l (KJV), and says that if they don't work, then they shouldn't eat (or not be allowed to eat). In other words, get off your butt and get to work, a God is not going to supply your needs, it takes a persons' self effort. It was clearly stated that they weren't doing work because they were "disorderly" and "busybodies."

DELUSION: MIRACLES

One of the early contacts of Billy Meier was a woman named Asket from the DAL universe which is a parallel universe to our universe, the DERN universe. On February 3, 1953, she stated the following to Billy regarding miracles. She said "I hereby speak of the extraterrestrial race, which here, since ancient times, wants to attain supremacy over the Earth humanity and, accordingly, to always again unfold the glow and flame of the various religions and always new sects because only through that may they obtain their goal. For thousands of years they deceived the Earth human with religious "miracles" and "visions" of every kind, in order to maintain, and to yet further increase, the religious delusion." [177]

So we see here that the religious delusion of so-called miracles through the science of early extraterrestrials had a "WOW" effect which led them eventually into the delusions, called miracles in the Bible, to get them to a point of submission and deception. This leads us to ask a question. How would you feel if you were from a 3rd world country and a medical doctor gave a shot to someone and cured them of an illness that had for previous years taken the lives of hundreds of people? You would respond "that is a miracle!" No it's not; it was developed from the laboratory of American Scientists from a chemical (s).

The same was true with extraterrestrial scientists thousands of years ago who did things that would "WOW" mankind, as reported in this work in Contact Report #251, just like the genetic mutations that were carried out that altered mankind's DNA for positive and negative results. This is not only an explanation but also a warning because someday you may be confronted with extraterrestrials as Betty and Barney Hill did when they were abducted…or even as Harry S., a conservative fundamental Baptist, <u>had to admit</u> to the reality of a UFO that cut off all electricity in their car as it slowly passed over it…apparently checking them out, as I referred to in the beginning of this writing.

DELUSION: GOD HELPS THOSE WHO HELP THEMSELVES

And let's get off this often quoted phrase "God helps those who help themselves." There are thousands and thousands of people that try and help themselves but do not have the planning abilities, assets, self-confidence, self-esteem, physical abilities, academic skill and other qualities to "make it in life." Another great example are those from various religious and non-religious backgrounds that "make it" in life and do not avail themselves to a Christian God. They "made it" in life because they had self-determination and a "will" to go after a goal or dream of accomplishment. Most of the

---

[177] Billy Meier, "Askets Explanations Part 1," *They Fly*, February 3, 1953, http:// www. theyfly.com.

time we forget that there are religions in the world that people cling to in which there are poor and rich alike. They continue to starve because of lack of rain, poor ground for farming, lack of farming skills, lack of farming equipment and lack of water. God doesn't suddenly sink a well for them or drop farm machinery in their front yard. It takes the brotherhood of mankind to come together and help people in depressed areas to show them and supply them with what they need. This is applicable to not only climate depressed areas but to cities of all sizes, urban and rural areas. The needs are plenteous and widespread!

Delusion: Prayer

I have witnessed an explosive amount of pain in the lives of people as a former pastor and evangelist when the prayers of Christians are not answered or they didn't receive the so called blessings that others seem to have. When you become <u>educated</u> about the circuinstance, <u>rational</u> in the options and <u>logical</u> in the choice afforded…it's really not about a God that is an all-in-all, it's about you and what you choose to do on a moment by moment basis called "responsibility."

Let's look at some misconceptions about God that people practice. We hear people say "you're an answer to prayer" or "God must have sent you" when really someone who knew of the person's plight spoke to others and gave a suggestion to help the person in whatever need they had. The result was that once the need was made known, someone took it upon themselves to help the person in need. God had nothing to do with it!!!

Another misconception is healing. "We will pray that you'll be healed" when in reality chemicals and conditions in the body change to make it seem like healing through prayer took place but in reality it came down to medicines or procedures that finally kicked-in and afforded a healing of its own.

Yet another misconception is for protection. People will say, "I'll pray for your safety as you drive to work, home, vacation, birthday party or whatever the destination. Yet so many times I have seen so-called godly people end up severely injured or killed. Who are you going to sue for not being protected? A God…or the person who said they would pray for your safe trip?

Think about this for a moment, the planet is full of people and people make mistakes or errors at home, work, at play or wherever they may be. It is not the will of a God; it is your personal responsibility to the best of your ability to be safe by being careful and attentive in spite of the recklessness of others. A God will not step in and lift the auto being driven by a drunken individual so that you won't get hit head-on!

The *Goblet of the Truth* stated the following regarding the topic of prayer.[178]

Prayer—is false. Page 185, chapter 5:95 and page 187, chapter 5:97.

Prayer is false—because there is no God to pray to. Page 207, chapter 6:62; page 19, chapter 2:129; page 201, chapter 6:27; page 223, chapter 6:152.

Prayer—is a fantasy of confused people. See Page 327, chapter 11:49.

Prayer—is not directed to God (s), priests, false prophets or servants of a deity. Page 319, chapter 11:2; page 323, chapter11:27-28.

The same is true about meditation as Billy Meier stated briefly regarding an inquiry on November 25, 2001 to a gentleman who asked if meditation would heal a physical injury. Billy responded that meditation cannot be used for physical healing.[179]

Prayer is directed to your own inner world (consciousness) which means it is an intimate conversation between you and your inner spirit. In specific, "prayer is directed to the power of Creation or to the fragment of spirit in the human or to the material consciousness and the material unconsciousness, so that it stimulates active powers in us and brings them to effect. Whether a prayer is directed to the Creation, or to the material consciousness-form itself, the fragment of Creation-spirit in the human would be addressed and stimulated and the prayer would be effective through the good hope and the knowledge of the human that the spirit, through its power, truthfully imparts help."[180]

As prayer is directed inwardly for personal forgiveness of errors and change, **meditation** is directed outwardly in positive expressions of intent

---

[178]   Billy Meier, *Goblet of the Truth* (Canada: FIGU-Landsgruppe Canada, 2015).

[179]   Billy Meier, "Questions to Billy Meier—Answered," *They Fly,* November 25, 2001, h ttp://www. theyfly. com/gaia/ answers. html.

[180]   Billy Meier, "The Creation Itself is Your Spirit," January 22, 2005, http://gaia- guys.net/ CreationisSpirit.htm.

through the "emission of powerful and logical impulses, a positive polarity can be forged to counteract the negative "force field" surrounding the Earth much like a huge bell, which influences the terrestrial population and all nature. This negative force field was established, and continues to be entrenched, by several centuries of religious-sectarian, extremist and deteriorated terrestrial human thinking. To reverse this negative energy, therefore, the concept has been to produce dynamic "counter impulses," which the extraterrestrials would send to Earth via a telemeter disk hovering high above the Semjase-Silver-Star-Center, coupled with some other devices and the assistance of over 3.5 billion humans within the Plejaran federation. We, at FIGU, have since discovered that by initiating this action the concept has obviously proved to be successful. The specific meditation for world peace as spoken in the Lyran tongue is "**Saalome gam naan ben uurda, gan njjber asaala hesporoona! Peace be on Earth, and among all beings!**" [181] Please look up the footnote to see guidance on proper participation in the meditation.

Meditation can also be used in a general sense for personal inner growth, judgment, and understanding as well as clarity of thought, wisdom, self-esteem, positive consciousness and health. Billy Meier suggested 77 statements/short sentences a person can use for a positive conscious-attitude requiring five quiet minutes just a few times daily. [182]

We have all heard the various expressions of prayer such as "I will pray for (whatever the concern is, such as improved health, a job, safety on the road, and various materialistic needs whether they are daily or special situations)." If a prayer is answered, you will hear the individual make statements such as "God is faithful," or "God met my needs," and other similar responses. Yet if the prayer is not answered, the *scapegoat* response is made "Well, it must not have been God's will" so that God is not made out to be a liar.

How many times have Christian believers prayed with certainty according to Matt. 21:22, Mark 11:24, John 14:13, 1 John 5:14 (KJV), and several other references and not receive the answer they wanted, either

---

[181]   Billy Meier, "Explanation of the True Peace Symbol," January 1, 2016, http://www.figu.org/ch/verein/periodika/sonder-bulletin/2014/nr-76/ friedenssymbol.

[182]   Billy Meier, "Meditation from Clear Visibility," July 28, 2009, http://www.futureofmankind.co.uk/Billy_Meier/Meditation_from_Clear_Visibility_ (book).

in part or in whole? If the prayer is claimed as answered, there are "high fives" all through their church, yet if it isn't answered, there is a demeanor of quietness, and there is no bragging of answered prayer.

I have told the story many times of the young man in the hospital that was deathly ill. He had six friends composed of a Baptist, Christian Reformed, Jew, Muslim, Seventh-day Adventist, and Catholic. The disease was announced as terminal and the man's friends said they would pray for his recovery in earnest. A few days after the announcement of the terminal illness, the young man passed away. His friends came to the hospital and found the bed empty and with clean linen. They asked at the nurse's station where the young man had been taken, and the response was that he had passed away in the night.

The question here is "With all the prayer that was made on behalf of the young man, why weren't the prayers of his friends unanswered?"

Going back to the example of the young man who was ill in the hospital and looking at it from the standpoint that the man was healed, the next question is "Whose deity/God would receive the credit for healing?" And if the man had died, could the finger of faithlessness be pointed at any or all of the man's friends for a lack of faith? A lack of action by their God?

In reviewing the definition of God earlier in this writing, we find that God is nothing more than a human of advanced technological and scientific knowledge and expertise. His power in the matters of men is limited to the laws of the universe…essentially what he can and cannot produce or make happen with the wisdom of material and scientific invention. So anything beyond his ability will rest with the expression "it was not God's will" or be accepted as the "Law of Cause and Effect."

Man has been led into the delusion of the power of prayer through written and verbal pronouncement. Prayer is called "faith-gambling" because if you win, you tell every one of your winnings/answered prayer. Yet if you don't win, you walk away hurt and sad, especially if you lay in your hospital bed with a terminal disease and all the prayers and laying-on of hands with oil does nothing for you.

Now to be fair in this subject, there have been those that have physically been partially or totally healed, but this has been through internal chemical changes and suggestive consciousness-power of the human being as stated in the *Talmud of Immanuel,* chapter 8, pages 142-166.

A foundational understanding regarding prayer can be found in the *Talmud of Immanuel,* chapter 21, pages 328-332, whereby one's own moral and psychical state are achieved. In specific, as quoted in the *Talmud of Immanuel* explanation on page 332, "In truth, it is solely the causal foreordinations that arise from the course of the relevant events and situations, etc. which then become erroneously and confusedly interpreted and misunderstood by the believers of cults, religions, and sects as 'their prayers and faith becoming heard.'"

DELUSION: GOD'S WILL

Did you ever do something, no matter how big or small, and later ask yourself "why did I do that? I felt that I was doing God's will for my life but the whole thing fell through! I felt in my heart that I was doing as God wanted me to!" Christians rush to carry the banner of Proverbs 3:5-6 (KJV) of trusting in the Lord and waiting for him to "direct thy paths" when in essence this is nothing more than a God bringing humankind under the control of God. This has happened over the thousands of years where advanced humans came to earth with the title of JHWHZ (God) and ruled earth humans with a heavy hand. In the year 2080 B.C. there was a ruler (JHWH/God) known as Kamagol the First who forced all earthly religions into his control and created terrible cults which demanded human blood, which were able to partially be maintained until the present."[183]

DELUSION: GOD IS ALL IN ALL

Another Delusion of Religion is the claim that God is omnipotent and can do as he pleases. This is totally false. Creation is energy, spirit-energy,[184] and when Creation created all the laws of life, whether physics, quantum mechanics, thermodynamics, geophysics, etc., a God cannot interfere with the creative processes and the established laws that determine the moment by moment life and the set function of each of the laws of science.

---

[183]   Billy Meier, "Contact 70," *They Fly,* January 6, 1977, http://www.theyfly.com/.

[184]   Billy Meier, "What is Creation?" *Stimme der Wassermannzeit,* no. 89 (December 1993).

These laws of science will eternally exist and all life on this planet or others must comply with its structure. Yes, the Destroyer Comet in 8104 B.C. wreaked havoc world-wide, but not a single law of science was broken…events acted due to one law of science "in concert" with another which made further laws of science come into play resulting in destruction through each of the applicable laws of science.

During the encounter with the Destroyer Comet of 8104 B.C., the poles of the earth shifted and the effects were that the equator changed due to the tilt of the earth.[185] From the effects of that Comet, the earth is where it is at in the tilt of its axis and its rotation. This was previously explained in the discussion of the Destroyer Comet of 8104 B.C. The bottom line is that God is just a human of advanced knowledge and abilities in the areas of science and cannot violate the laws of life that are established by creation.

DELUSION: A DEITY CIRCUMVENTING THE LAWS OF CREATION

All creational positive and negative effects are based on the laws of various fields of science. Their resulting affect is called Cause and Effect and can be observed in our daily lives. In fact, an example can be seen in the Bible, in I Kangs, chapter 18, (KJV). In this incident, which called for a challenge between the gods of Baal and the God of Israel, the description on how the altar for the sacrifice was the same except for Elijah's scheme which included stone (burnt limestone which made "quicklime," the offering of oxen coated with gold (sulfur), and then the pouring of water on the whole setup. This combination of quicklime plus sulfur and burnt limestone (known in ancient times as "instant fire,") ignited in just a matter of minutes making it appear as if the God of Israel had accomplished a miracle.[186] See also Mischa V. Alyea's "Fire from Water: The Way of the True God According to Elijah.[187]

---

[185] Billy Meier, "Contact 248," *They Fly,* February 3, 1994, http://www.theyfly. com/.

[186] Wikipedia, s.v. "Petroleum Naphtha," accessed February 12, 2019, https:// en.wikipedia. org/wiki/Petroleum_naphtha.

[187] Mischa V. Alyea, " Fire from Water: The Way of theTrue God According to Elij ah," July 28, 2013, https://jesusweddingthebook.wordpress.com/2013/07/28/

One of the biggest delusions in Christianity is the belief in a God (deity) that exhibits a character in time past that is active in the lives of mankind.

DELUSION: THAT THE BIBLE DOESN'T SAY ANYTHING ABOUT UFO

Many scholars of the Bible try and tell the public that there is no reference in the Bible regarding UFO, therefore there is no such thing as a UFO nor aliens from other planets. That's like saying that since automobiles weren't invented in the 1700's that there can be no automobile. Words and terminologies are invented every year that no one has thought-up because many of those terminologies are related to inventions that had not been in existence before. So if we want to be strict on this issue, as others that say there are no UFO or aliens, we could rightfully say that if a subject isn't in the dictionary in the 1700's, then it doesn't exist.

For those that hold onto the statement that "if UFO and aliens are not in the Bible, then they don't exist," it shows a very narrow-mindedness and the proven fact that they have a delusion that permeates their thinking to such an extent that they are blinded by the truth. Although there are cases where UFO sightings are a hoax or the possibility of a country testing skills in the development of spacecraft, there are still a fair number of "actual" sightings that exist and have been documented on internet sites such as and the National UFO Reporting Center at.

In addition to these organizations mentioned above is my personal testimony at the beginning of this work which I briefly state here as witnessing UFO flyovers approximately 400 ft. above me or myself and my wife and witness, flashing back of UFO that we are flashing light at, and on one occasion a UFO hovering about 8-10 ft. above the ground just 300 feet from my wife and I. On one particular flyover I was able to get a picture of the underside of one UFO as it flew overhead.

Some of the greatest delusions that Religionists hold onto are statements and concepts that aren't in the Bible. They claim that UFO are not in the Bible and make their claim that if the idea of UFO and aliens are not in the

---

fire- from-water-the-way-of-the-true-god/.

Bible, then it cannot be true. Yet I would point out to them that there are many words not in the Bible even though the concept of what those words mean are in the Bible. Remember, people in Old and New Testament times described events, experiences and people in the terms that "they knew" according to their culture and knowledge of everyday life and the little technology they had…not ours!

There are many other terms that are not in the Bible that by some metamorphosis gives people the idea that they are in the Bible, such as "angels having wings, the devil as having horns and a pitchfork, birth control, an apple in the Garden of Eden (just fruit), a "whale" that swallowed Jonah, that Jesus was single, additional words not in the Bible i.e. gambling, liturgy, age of accountability, abortion, transgender and many other terms.[188]

What Do I Follow?

Back in the 1950's, UFOlogy was barely spoken of, but it was introduced in the term of "UFO". When UFO sightings and reports started to appear in the news media it was as if fear was stuck in the hearts of mankind! But who would connect the dots to Biblical history? Or wasn't there a connection? What interested me in my 30's was a book published in 1986 titled *The Mystery Clouds* by Dr. Donald P. Coverdell, Th.D. Could he have introduced a theological explanation to UFOlogy? Was it true in part or in whole?

After Dr. Coverdell wrote his book in 1986, I was baffled and left the subject alone while I completed my Masters' and Doctorate in Religious Education with a major in Christian Education and Apologetics. I had been an Evangelist for Campsite Evangelism for several years and did pastoring in Michigan and later in Pennsylvania. When not in pastoring, I was teaching Biblical subjects in a local Christian Institute in Salt Lake City, Utah, as well as teaching in a local Christian Church. In pastoral circles no one dared to mention a relationship or connection of the Bible to UFO.

In 2014, I delved into UFOlogy more through the book *Light Years* by Gary Kinder, the story of Billy Meier and his contacts from a planet beyond the Pleiades. My wife and I left Christianity in early 2016 and

---

[188]   David Householder, "Surprising Things Not Found in the Bible; How Many Can You Guess?" accessed February 18, 2019, http://www.christianpost.com/ news/67/surp rising- things-not-found-in-the-bible-how-many-can-you-giess. html.

we began using light code to communicate with UFO. Would I describe seeing UFO as those in Old and New Testament times? My wife and I remember how a UFO would show itself as a distant white light that suddenly came on. It would become bigger as it came toward us…and then flew over us, only to disappear in the blink of an eye as it left our dimension and went into another dimension. If I were in Old or New Testament times and describing our experiences of flyovers and close encounters I would probably say in their limited vocabulary that it was like a meteor, but without a glowing tail.

On one particular night time, one of my students from a class that I teach regarding the Billy Meier story was standing next to me late in the evening when a UFO flew about 50 feet above the tree- tops a short distance away. I pulled out my night vision binoculars and was able to see the UFO from the side at which time I plainly saw the cab on top of it…. just the way I had seen it in a UFO encounter my wife and I had just 300 ft. from us hovering a few feet above the ground. O.K., how would you describe it in the vocabulary of those in the Old Testament times? Probably as a bowl shaped object, a very bright glow to it with a top that was like a bubble with windows around it!

Truth in Interpretation, Transinterpretation, and Reality

With that said, let's look at a particular example in the Bible. The text that I have chosen is 2 Kings 2:11 (KJV). We have to keep in mind that we need to look at the text through the eyes of the supposed writer of 2 Kings, Jeremiah.

There are times that Biblical Scripture has to be interpreted in the strictest sense such as in ceremonies, conversations and events. There are other times that an interpreter can, what I call, *transinter- pretate* a word or phrase for clearer or functional understanding.

So as we look at 2 Kings 2:11 (KJV), the first word that needs to be *transinterpretated* is the word for *chariot*. The word *chariot,* first of all, is not capitalized, and in its general sense is a mode of transportation. The second word of interest is the word *fire.* At this point, it would raise a person's eyebrows if a chariot was on fire, but there was nothing in the verse to suggest that it was actually burning up and resulting in a pile of ashes. Now keeping that in mind, we approached another weird spectacle called *horses of fire*. Keep in mind that scribes used what vocabulary was at hand, and when we look at the Hebrew meaning of horses of fire it is not to be translated in the context of actual horses, but "as the sound of horses" That is to say, the sound of a flying machine which would make the roar of horses running as if they were on fire or driven by fire. If these were actual horses with an actual open chariot, the riders and horses would never survive due to the eventual altitude and result in the passenger fainting and dying as well as the horses. The whirlwind at the end of the verse is simply the rush of air from engines that gave the space ship propulsion for either vertical or horizontal ascent into the sky.

The verse now would read "And it came to pass, as they still went on, and talked, that behold there appeared a space ship glowing as if on fire, and the loud sound of its engines was that of running horses that were driven by fire; Elijah then boarded the craft and the ship departed with a rush of air from its engines into the sky."

The same application of transinterpretation can be applied when reviewing Ezekiel chapter 1 (KJV) where we can clearly see the descending of a wheel within a wheel in a horizontal form with another horizontal smaller wheel inside it with spokes going from the small horizontal wheel to the larger one. The living creatures depicted in Ezekiel chapter 1 (KJV) are creatures that have had genetic manipulation applications as stated in Contact Report 202.[189]

There were many famous religious paintings in the 1300s, 1400s, 1500s, 1600s, and 1700s that depicted UFOs called *The Crucifixion of Christ* (1350); *The Baptism of Christ* (1710); *The Madonna with Saint Giovannino* (late 1400s); *Israel, Put Your Hope in the* Zonf painting (circa 1600s); *Triumph of Summer tapestry* (1538); *Glorification of the Eucharist* (early 1600s); *The Crucifixion of Christ (area* 1600s); *Foppa Adorazione* (1478); and *Egyptian Pictograph* (400 B.C.). The question that comes to mind is "why would the UFO be part of the painting unless it was really seen?" Of special note is when you enlarge the picture of *The Crucifixion Of Christ* (1350), look at the upper left and right hand corners because

---

[189]   Billy Meier, "Contact 202," *They Fly,* August 24, 1985, http://www.theyfly. com/.

you will unmistakably see two small UFO with a man seated in each of them.[190] This is similar to the transinterpretation of 2 Kings 2:11 (KJV).

Let's stop here and ask a question. Why is it that a person never hears about these paintings in a sermon or Bible lesson? Because they would lose their following of people! Why? Because their attention would be diverted to the mysterious past of the Old and New Testament Times of what the Bible portrays or more correctly should portray. It would also cause confusion as to the existence and purpose of a God, throw doubt on the dogmas of Christianity and cause a financial collapse in all areas of religious activities due to a lack of credibility in the church and what it stands for.

A question was asked of Billy Graham once which was in regards to the possibility of UFO in the Bible. Billy Graham answered the "Bible does not say anything about UFO or the possibility of life on other planets."[191]

Billy Graham lived from November 7, 1918 to February 21, 2018. He certainly knew about UFO existing by means of others testifying of visual observation either of flying or landing as well as people being abducted by UFO. So to say that they are not in the Bible or the possibility of life on other planets is to say they don't exist at all. It's either you do accept the fact that UFO exist or you don't! And when there is clear testimony of UFO and yet a person dogmatically says they don't exist here or anywhere else is committing (in teaching of Christianity) a sin by blatantly denying reality." Pope Francis claims the same thing as does Billy Graham, but Pope Francis also said something that proves the point.

He said, "Honestly, I wouldn't know how to answer."

Yet at least he was open enough to caution people not to count UFOs out because he further stated, "Until America was discovered, we thought it didn't exist, and instead, it existed."[192]

---

190 Tom Carlson, "Ten Historical Paintings That Prove Aliens Have Already Visited Us in the Past," *Boredom Therapy*, accessed February 18, 2019, http:// boredomtherapy.com/ paintings-with-ufos/.

191 Billy Graham, "Aliens Archives: Billy Graham Evangelistic Association," accessed February 18, 2019, https://billygraham.org/answer/bible-say- anything-life-planets/.

192 Elise Harris, "Do Aliens Exist? Pope Francis Tackles This (and Other Things) in New Interview," October 15, 2015, https://www.catholicnewsagency.com/ news/do-aliens-exist-pope-francis-tackles-this-and-other-things-in-new-in ter- view-75 02 5.

The question lay in whether Christianity had been "rightly dividing the word of truth" (2 Timothy 2:15, KJV), or lying about it to cover up the real biblical truth and promote their own agenda.

Here is a perfect example of the blindness of Christians to biblical interpretation as it relates to real-life explanation. People can become so blind, as I once was as a Christian evangelist and pastor, that we forget that we are living in a world of reality and to not acknowledge a very blatant reality such as the existence of UFOs is a Christian sin. That would be like stating there is no such thing as the word *tornado* (which by the way is another example of a word that's not in the Bible), and yet driving down your street and seeing a tornado blow your house away yet stating that it was not a tornado because you took a dogmatic, unrealistic, and lying stance that everyone else in the area witnessed and attested to the fact that your home was indeed destroyed by a tornado.

A recent Georgetown study stated that religion has an estimated worth of $1.2 trillion in the US economy. This is not only through the church collection plate but also through and in support of all auspices of religious activity and endeavors.[193] Can you imagine the hit that the US economy would take if everyone stopped giving to their own respective religious organization or cause? This is also confirmed by the Religious Freedom and Business Foundation.[194]

So where do we go from here?

When interpretation is made of any type of writings, etchings, symbols, etc., the values of what it was in the original form must be correct. Where understanding of its meaning is needed to complete the conveyance of the message, there must be the careful yet realistic communication of its message through transinterpretation as described earlier in this work. What that means is that the story, event, or news must be transferred from the crude and simple way the writer was seeing, hearing, and experiencing things to the present-day understanding while keeping an open mind toward developing a realistic context.

---

[193]   Lauretta Brown, "Georgetown Study: Religion Worth $1.2 Trillion in US Economy, More Than Google and Apple Combined," September 16, 2016, http://www.cnsnews.com.

[194]   Brian J. Grim, "Religion May Be Bigger Business Than We Thought," *Religious Freedom and Business Foundation,* accessed February 18, 2019, https://www. weforum.org/ agenda/2017/01/religion-bigger-business-than-we-thought/.

CONCLUSION

This book was not meant to bash anyone's beliefs. It was meant to (1) open the view of past history, (2) advise the reader of chronological errors of world events, (3) challenge the reader to assess their present faith in light of a higher and more complete revelation of the events of the universe and in particular the Earth, and (4) to introduce to mankind the actual and proven existence of advanced humans, namely the Plejaren, that have revealed themselves to and through their chosen ambassador, "Billy" Eduard A. Meier.

The teachings of Christianity and other religions hinder us from understanding our human beginnings and heritage on Earth as well as understanding the history of the Universe in full measure. Religious institutions teach only what they say is between the covers of what is called the Bible.

Let me pose a question at this point to what I call the "religionists." Why not admit the truth and integrate the legacy, which the Plejarens have left us, into Biblical history?

It is "high time" that we pull the covers back on the bed of delusion we have slept in for many years and see that humans from other areas of the Universe have come to Earth many times and have been instrumental in our history.

Those particular times are not only recorded in rock inscriptions, tales of visitors from the stars, recorded on paper or other writing material, but also amazingly in the Bible. They are recorded in instances when so-called miracles occurred, people disappeared or re-appeared, a voice from the sky, appearances of smoke or fire in the sky and people were carried away by a flying object means of transportation.

Now, it's time for you to "look outside the box!"

ABOUT THE AUTHOR

Dr. Ron Pleune was born in Grand Rapids, Michigan and has earned a Bachelor in Business Administration from Aquinas College, Grand Rapids, Michigan, and a Master's and Doctorate in Christian Education with a major in Apologetics from Bethany Theological Seminary, Dothan, Alabama. Dr. Pleune is also a Certified Behavior Management Specialist and Certified Security Supervisor/ Manager.

Dr. Pleune's career focused on Business Management positions as well as several years as a campground evangelist and in the pastorate. Just before retirement in 2015, Dr. Pleune and his wife became acquainted with a book titled *Light Years* by Gary Kinder, which introduced them to the *Goblet of the Truth* and the Contact Reports from the Plejaren who had initially contacted Billy Eduard A. Meier in 1942, at the age of five years old. Several years later, Billy Meier began his mission to teach others the "Truth" through the Teaching of the Laws and Recommendations (the laws of science and the positive living and treatment of mankind and the Earth itself).

Dr. Pleune and his wife researched the matter thoroughly and in the early spring of 2016 left the Christian faith. Dr. Pleune developed and directs Living Truth Fellowship where he teaches the Billy Meier story and the Teachings of the Truth along with general UFOlogy. Dr. Pleune is also directly responsible for developing the *Goblet of the Truth* index for Billy Meier, which can be viewed on the website http://www.theyfly.com/. The index is a list of topics in the *Goblet of the Truth* that facilitates easy access for personal growth.

Dr. Pleune teaches a nine-week seminar on the Billy Meier story along with some UFOlogy at various locations and also presents a one-and-a-half-hour introductory presentation at libraries and other entities regarding UFOlogy and the Billy Meier story. Please contact Dr. Pleune for speaking or teaching presentations at drpleune@gmail.com.

www.ingramcontent.com/pod-product-compliance
Lightning Source LLC
Chambersburg PA
CBHW040231170726
48295CB00014B/876